Rebelling Like There's No Tomorrow

Sue Hampton

TSL Publications

First published in Great Britain in 2023
By TSL Publications, Rickmansworth

Copyright © 2023 Sue Hampton

ISBN: 978-1-915660-34-3

Cover courtesy of : Sue Hampton

Contents

Introduction

I'm now less of a small author than a small activist very aware that other climate protesters have taken bolder and more regular action and spent more time in prison. Like *Rebelling for Life* which documented my XR year in 2020, and *Still Rebelling for Life*, a second collection of short stories, personal accounts and poems from 2021, *Rebelling Like There's No Tomorrow* grew from activism – this time through 2022, a year that extended my criminal record with Just Stop Oil as well as Extinction Rebellion and took me, briefly, to HMP Bronzefield.

It's been a year in which climate protest has regenerated around the world, temperatures have decimated records and floods, fires and droughts should rationally have raised the alarm more effectively than sitting in a road or throwing soup at the glass protecting a painting. Scientists agree that climate chaos is increasing faster than their models predicted and some are taking to the streets themselves, because still governments subsidise fossil fuels and sign off new oil, gas and coal projects that make a mockery of the Paris Agreement. Time is short. Like them I don't know what, other than nonviolent civil disobedience, can force change from criminal governments hell-bent on endangering life on this planet.

This book won't raise much money to fund direct action, and I don't kid myself that it will reach more than a few hundred readers. But maybe just a few of those will feel stirred to play a more determined part in the movement for climate, racial and social justice.

blog post from March 2022

Bad character

Recently, two years after my last author-in-school visit, a teacher from a comprehensive asked if she could book me for a Diversity and Inclusion Day. There was a time when I would have been delighted to raise awareness about alopecia as well as the power of stories, but that's changed. For a start, having read widely through lockdown about racism, white privilege and fragility, and having protested against a bill that criminalises the Romany and traveller community (and reported Jimmy Carr to Twitter), I can't help feeling that challenging as it is, alopecia rates relatively low on the disadvantage and discrimination list. I volunteered for six years with a refugee charity; I have a Deaf friend and others with transgender children. My beloved husband is non-binary. So while I haven't forgotten how diminished and fearful alopecia made me for nearly three decades, as an ambassador for diversity I'd feel something of a fraud as a middle-class white woman who no longer minds being bald and blames a superficial consumer and celebrity culture. But of course, the education was always about respect and empathy rather than hair. So I would have accepted the booking, except that the teacher who made contact believed me to be an Ambassador for Alopecia UK and I'm not, not any more, by mutual agreement, to spare the charity grief, because I'm a "person of bad character" according to the Crown Prosecution Service. The government's endless climate crimes have made a criminal of me.

I have an XR sweatshirt with FREE THE TRUTH on the back, thanks to the action at Newsprinters in Broxbourne that led to my name being printed among others in the *Daily Mail* and *Telegraph*. Before that last pre-Covid school visit I emailed about my convictions, the Head never replied to the teacher concerned and the staff apparently cheered my lawbreaking at their morning briefing, but I couldn't assume another blind eye being turned and a UKIP candidate once made such an abusive media fuss about me talking for the refugee charity in assembly at his child's primary that the Head had to involve the governors and finally let the parents decide whether my invitation stood. Which it did, although I watched the door in the hall. But in later life I have shifted identity from ex-Head Girl once nominated for Teacher of the Year (while pretending to be normal under a wig), to an author booked by some 600 schools to a persona non grata, and now to a troublemaker likely to stir up controversy as a climate and peace activist. For the first time in my life, I'm in a minority that is more than merely hated by some and ridiculed by others. If only schools would let me, I'd rather focus on the greatest crisis in history. Yet a friend was accused by a Deputy Head of radicalising her daughter by accompanying her to the first Rebellion. And it's not so long since Prevent listed XR as a terrorist organisation and asked teachers to report such cases. It's all bonkers – especially when Greta graces hundreds of school walls. But the truth is, the facts about climate change are not taught as they should be, even at a time when pupils' lives will according to the science be overwhelmed and threatened by the crisis around which the curriculum only skirts. Our right wing media has ensured that attempts to teach the truth about Britain's colonial history are considered political and woke and Black Lives Matter can't be presented in class as valid protest. The government, it seems, wants the reality we all need to live by kept conveniently out of our classrooms as well as the headlines.

So I freed the truth about my arrests in my reply to this school's enquiry, using words like love and conscience as well as nonviolence. My email was passed on to the Head who declined to take the risk I represent, or have to manage complications. I wasn't surprised. When activism became my priority I knew writing must come second and that without paid bookings I would be left with a lot of stock on my shelves. I feel a little sadness, and I don't deny the buzz when kids were excited to see me – "Sue Hampton's here!" – or the ego boost of a long queue at the signing table after school. I hope I made an impact when I shared my themes of love, understanding, courage and freedom and made reading and writing fun. I did some writer-in-residence projects that felt truly worthwhile. I tell myself I'm also spared the humiliation served up on those infrequent but memorable occasions when no student knew I was coming, teachers worked on laptops during my presentations, no one spoke to me at lunchtime and I prepared my author table only to pack up again with the vegan ice cream money tub weighing pretty much the same.

I recently decided to donate all my earnings to Extinction Rebellion – at a point when those earnings have plummeted with no hope of recovery. I no longer expect to be booked for World Book Day two or three years ahead. My name is Sue Hampton, I've written over forty books and I'm an activist now.

poem from March 2022

Heading for Extinction

Pale and unassuming among shoots,
the irises take me by surprise,
until the grape hyacinths and the knopfia
risen from sleet.
There are letterboxes that mangle truth,
and others where warning words drift free
to alarm on tiles or carpet.
Small rainbow wellingtons on doormats
make me hope Extinction's
harder to read
than SUVs and Union Jacks and labelled threats.
I'm smiling on the leaflet
and the word LOVE is bold and red
but I'm a bearer of bad news,
as welcome as a bailiff,
and I'm sorry,
sorry the media didn't break it first,
sorry to wake the sleeping with a rude alarm.
Sorry for the message
Peace be with you,
but please come along to hear facts
that you will never escape again,
that will lodge deep and engulf the rest.
The guilt disturbs.
But careful maintenance
solid assets and well-mannered borders
sew doubt.
To embrace resistance
of the civil, law-breaking kind,
is to shift identity,
lose society's respect,
strip the value of everything else.
Is to cry.
Is to fear.

Is to cast around for hope.
I wish you didn't need to know
But you do.
The world does, and must.
Read or unread, however it made you feel,
this leaflet is an act of love.

blog post from April 2022, published in May by The Friend

Risk-taking

Last Sunday, in Quaker Meeting, a wonderful woman called Marjorie, who is 91, *gave ministry* about risk. She didn't actually use the word, but she spoke of elderly Ukrainian women not only standing peacefully in front of Russian soldiers but talking to them, on behalf of their mothers. Moved as I pictured this scene, I remembered a tweet I'd seen an hour or two earlier from Peter Kalmus, @ClimateHuman, a climate scientist whose grief and passion is always palpable: I'm often asked, *"What can I do?"* or *"How can I be a climate activist?" Answer: Take risks. There's a lot of guidance you can get, groups you can join, advice you can seek. But it won't amount to much, if anything, if you don't take risks.*

I'd taken a risk that weekend by gluing myself to Barclays St Albans in protest at the ever-increasing funding of fossil fuels by Europe's dirtiest bank, been arrested, strip-searched and charged with criminal damage (although superglue comes off with nail varnish remover). It was a risk I understood and a relatively predictable outcome. I'm committed to such risk taking – emotional, financial and physical – in an attempt to protect Planet Earth and all its life. But most concerned humans are unwilling. Risk can be a powerful deterrent, and in XR we understand the potential cost of activism, which goes deep psychologically. For those of us who have always tried to be good and nice, approved and liked, through school and work and beyond, as a full-time business, there's fear of losing that respectable identity, and a sense of loss once it's been compromised by trouble-making. I feel that loss, just a little, even after three and a half years. I was the girl who had nightmares at school about the detentions I was never given.

There's something bigger, though, and more powerful: the risk of broken relationships with those we love most. It must be exhausting and painful for anyone living with someone who doesn't understand or agree with their commitment, or the level of it, or its expression. Someone who believes that the activist's primary devotion is no longer to them – perhaps even that their marriage vows are being broken. Someone who considers their activism misguided, or dangerous. Too great a risk to that person they love, and the connection between them. I know Rebels in this situation and it must be acutely painful, a constant dilemma, a cause of friction and separation. Those in Insulate Britain who risked prison as well as the vitriol and contempt of the majority couldn't know, when they sat on their first motorway, how much they would lose. Some served a couple of weeks, others a few months. I hope every one of them felt loved through the experience, which is hard to anticipate emotionally and imaginatively before sentencing.

Would I risk prison? It's almost impossible to answer, and I believe that risk both worth taking and beyond my personal capacity, with an outcome I fear but could also endure and survive. But what of Mum, 94? What of my beloved husband, older and more fragile than me? What of my children, who support me but for whom this might be a step too far, and my grandchildren for whom I will soon be caring once a week? What if my relationships with these people I love are weakened by my decision at their expense? What of my bowels; my vegan, gluten-free diet; my depression and need of company? What if I just cry through each day and night?

Those protesting in Russia risk their liberty for peace. In Ukraine, the women talking to the *enemy* soldiers about their mothers risk their lives. So here, however much we regret the slide into authoritarianism evidenced by the Crime, Police and Sentencing Bill, we have it easy. No climate protester is likely to be shot (even though I did consider that possibility when I saw the heavily armed militarism of the Lord Mayor's Show where a few of us from Christian Climate Action intervened). How much risk we are prepared to take may depend on a number of factors, like age and employment, social status, health, our life experience, the information we've accessed, the attitude of our friends and family and, inescapably, our own individual temperament. At Barclays on Friday, all bar one of our little group of Rebels identified as introverts, so shyness and lack of confidence are not apparently a barrier to action. None of the activists I know had been in trouble with the police before their first arrest with XR, so being a lifelong law-abiding citizen does not in itself prevent people taking that first alarming step of arrestable activity. The question then is what, psychologically, differentiates the risk-takers from the bystanders, many of whom must also according to the polls be concerned, or very concerned, about climate change. I wish I knew the answer, and the wish is more fervent year on year as time runs out and emissions continue to rise while weather events around the world grow more extreme.

Those I've called bystanders may of course be taking action of a different sort, with their local Transition Town, or in local politics where the green agenda is, at least at face value, acceptable. Skill sets clearly influence our choices as much as temperament and the two may be intertwined. For a long time I saw myself as a keyboard warrior, weaving eco themes and climate chaos into my fiction as an author, originally for children and YA. It wasn't enough. Neither were the changes I made as a flight-free vegan trying to shop zero waste, bank ethically and use a renewable energy provider. One COP after another failed to deliver climate justice for those nations most at risk and least to blame, and pledges proved empty. Desperation made me a Rebel willing to deal with arrest and the courtroom. Desperation and love. Because as Gail Bradbrook said and I like to quote repeatedly, "We can only protect those closest to us when we remember our love for those furthest away." Desperation, love and faith as a Quaker who has always tried to follow Jesus. I might have assumed that people of faith are more likely to take risks that may involve sacrifice, and there are many in the climate and peace movements, probably representing a higher percentage than outside. But religious people are nonetheless divided on nonviolent direct action, with some relying on divine intervention and others simply seeing NVDA as a step too far, especially if it causes any kind of disruption – which protest is designed to do if it is to have any impact at all. XR is beyond politics, but there are plenty of Rebels who tried that as a route to change before growing impatient with progress.

There is no average Rebel and no obvious determining factor that overrides concerns to make us risk takers. The best I can offer is not simply accepting or knowing the climate science but taking its meaning deep into the heart, soul, mind and core. Once embedded, it's overwhelming and can't be removed. But there may still be other considerations that prevent activism. I'm doing what I can to appeal to people I know through blogs, videos and emails, and face to face, because there's a theory of social change that says we need 3.5% of the population to rebel to effect change. We all modify our behaviour in the light of what those in our social circles say and do. The risks we will be taking in the Rebellion are tiny set against the courage of peacemakers in Ukraine and Russia. They are dwarfed by the risk to livelihood, health and life with which millions in the Global South already struggle thanks to climate change. The cost of protest has become less predictable and is already on the rise. But as humans we take risks anyway: falling in love, crossing the road, cycling or driving, becoming parents, eating a product past its sell-by date, leaving the umbrella at home, quitting one job for another, relying on last-minute prep or revision, accepting another glass of wine or frequenting the chip shop, not making contact, delaying troubling the doctor, booking anything in advance. Saying yes or saying no. The risks Peter Kalmus had in mind are different, though, because they're not prompted by convenience or self-interest. And unless enough of us really, actively try to save the world, by telling the truth and serving it, the consequences will be catastrophic.

poem written in April 2022

JUST STOP OIL: below the beacon, Buncefield Oil Depot

The ship sailed dim and early,
its pale sea of concrete breaking into night-blurred fields.
Now I'm on a tarmac deck
watching a netted hammock that swings with limbs
beneath an orange swell
sculpted and reworked by wind.
Long bamboo masts
criss-cross to rise,
and the tepee tip marks an indigo black
that waits to streak banner-bright,
as a chill dawn silhouettes officers
like shadow puppets
in freeze-frame.

The layers that bulked to slow my run
still a shiver inside
but soon the ceiling's blue,
a seagull's curious as the drone,
and laser heat targets
my sliver of unprotected skin…
Now all seethes ashen grey
that advances till it occupies,
casting snowflakes
to melt on lips like sugar,
and foil-cased feet must clash before they set.

That's the way of it,
my day of sky,
my right arm reaching deep into a metal tube.
When I dislodge my rucksack pillow
Imodium allows me snacks.
When my friend tips me water
a nappy dares me drink.
I could be a patient in a hospital bed

but the drama's above me,
where gusts assault,
and the thin legs tremble
like a giraffe's from a wound.

My composition restored, I find for now
the climbers' faith.
On the tanker, and beneath,
it's a lock-on life
while police come and go
like extras on re-takes,
and decisions are made
at a level said to be high.
Time scuds like cloud.
Into the scene voices hurl
the science without response
that brings us here.
But our uniformed audience
has no comment to make.
By afternoon the crew in black
offer goggles, cut me free for arrest.
Scalp briefly bared, I'm remembered.
"You haven't learned," he smiles.
"Or I haven't."
The van leaves our climbers behind,
but we know
it's just a matter of time.

poem written in April 2022

Queen Elizabeth Playing Fields, with Joshua

I know the places
where the surface crumbles
and your wheels falter
but you don't stir.
The flower bed I cross for
regenerates without drama,
no trace of hyacinths' perfume glut
on the catwalk of tulips' chic.
And then, with you tilted for sleep and shade,
lips apart and one hand holding on,
we're there again, for yet more circuits,
dogs and buggies, Red Kites above
and layered pensioners on tennis courts.
This Nature's urban-bare,
humanised and neutered
for limited function.
With throb and grind,
with brick dust and shifted earth,
new streets encroach on green
but I choose trees that veil them
where birds still sing.
Sometimes, naming, seeing,
the time we take feels bright,
so safe with prayer,
with wraparound now,
that I'm held
not by love for brave or giving strangers,
nor heady circus time I used to serve
but this, only this,
with you.

not exactly a story

April 2022

Oil Terminal by Night

It was hard, in the rural darkness, to negotiate the uneven earth or avoid the brambles that half-blocked the pathway from the narrow lane into the field. The illuminated steel blocks and cylinders that made the oil terminal rose ahead at the furthest point she could see, grimly out of place beyond trees and hedges. Since for her maps and directions had never communicated much, she hadn't looked or listened actively, trusting in the judgement of those who'd investigated that everyone would be able to manage the physical challenges. She'd positioned herself towards the end of the thin black line advancing along the edge of the field so as not to delay younger and more agile bees, and when the first obstacle emerged out of the night, in the form of a wire fence, she watched those in front of her throw seriously bulky backpacks ahead of them in order to press down and climb through the middle, or straddle over the top. As she chose the gap, bent and accepted a guiding hand, she realised this would be like a tube journey, except that instead of offering her their seat the men from later decades would feel obliged to assist the elderly with support, encouragement and whatever pulling, pushing and hoiking was necessary. And looking at the steep slope that faced her now, and the bodies scrambling up to the sound of earth and stones falling away behind them, she thought hoiking might soon be essential.

As she began to climb she felt it crumble, some of it as soft as sand but with flints sharp enough to scrape and thump. Not so much a hill or cliff as a slag heap. People were holding on to the thin trunk of a tree that could slide away too, like the bank that subsided in *The Railway Children*. It didn't help much, and however carefully she placed her feet there were no footholds that actually held. Falling onto her stomach she slipped downwards, but someone above was reaching down for her, and she dismissed thoughts of being a liability. She wasn't the oldest senior citizen after all, just a child who'd been afraid of heights, the gym and cross-country running. And dirt. Standing at the top of the slope she remembered paying attention to the assurance that the railway track she must step on wasn't electrified. Her Doc Martens could cope with this, scuffed as they were being dragged across the road by a police officer at the Lord Mayor's parade. But she realised she'd already lost her buddy, a primary school teacher of a similar age with whom she'd bonded, and didn't have much hope, without phones and in covert silence, of reuniting with her. Before long there was a gate, the lock of which had been broken so that it was held open for all-comers, but she saw with dismay that the next slope was downwards. The branch she decided might help turned out to be spiked with thorns. Taking the drop at a wild-boy run might get this over with sooner than slow and steady care.

Afterwards the sequence grew hazy. Did the long, wide horizontal pipes come next? In any case they were strong enough to take her eight stone – even though the kit-laden backpack with its dangling sleeping bag and the roll mat under her arm could bring her up to nine. A helicopter shone a searchlight that made them crouch, head down; its throbbing whine burst through the quiet like a threat. Which was almost funny because she'd scorned action movies, spies and chases for slow-burn love stories way back in her teens. But the fear and excitement meant adrenaline was working anyway.

Then the pipes made a high, not-quite-tessellated bank that could have been an installation. Never, ever, did she think she'd be doing this, anything like this. Even at twenty she would have stopped in her tracks: I can't. And at the top of it there was a steel fence separating them from the oil terminal – or rather, separating her and the few mature women behind her, because most of the team were already on site. The women said they couldn't manage it and would try to find another way in, but she didn't say that any more, not since she'd joined XR. She reminded herself that she'd climbed on top of a lorry opposite a magistrates' court and onto the roof of Barclays St Albans with a banner. Once she made a little progress up the pipes and estimated the fence at eight feet, someone pulled her on. A few more feet up and she was offered a knee to stand on. "Are you sure?" And then, with a shove from behind, a tug from above and someone to steady her landing on the other side, she was over.

Maybe if she'd looked at the map she'd have some idea what to do now. Telling herself she wasn't really alone, she walked in the direction she thought others had already gone, in the hope that she'd stumble on the loading bay. Making out figures ahead, she increased her walking pace and found two of the guys had waited to help her on her stomach through a hole, possibly recently opened, in a thin wire fence. A short flight of steps took her down after them into an area with a high roof and platforms that might be called gantries. She supposed this was the loading bay although she couldn't see any tankers to surf. Up to her left she saw some of the others, and recognised her buddy, already in position. Relieved, she climbed the metal stairway to join them, put down her heavy backpack and wondered what she could glue herself to, or whether she'd have to climb up into the pipes, or at least try.

In the debrief session at the safe house some twenty hours later she couldn't say which came first: the downpour or the shouts. Yellow-jacketed security guards down on the ground were running and yelling. Water was pounding down in torrents, the heaviest rain she'd ever known, so cold and hard and saturating all her layers so quickly that she felt helpless even before the men began to charge, swearing, up the steps. "It's not rain," someone said. "They've turned the sprinklers on us." Later, when she filed a complaint against the guards for assault, she couldn't say how many there were. Maybe four or five? And the one who threw her to the ground? She thought that must have happened from behind. There was so little narrative, just violence and the kind of verbal abuse that had never bombarded her before, not with such rage and hate, and she wondered as she fell near the steps whether she'd keep on tumbling down them. And one guy, the one who'd climbed the beacon at a different depot, had a cut eye, bruise swelling. As they were bundled forcibly out to the road around the site, he said he'd been kicked in the head when pushed to the ground.

"My bag's back there," she told every police officer she saw. "It's got everything in it." Debit card and keys; glasses and a favourite novel – *Housekeeping* – for the cell; medication, clean knickers. The cold was overwhelming through the wait that followed – for arrest after detention, for others to be delivered to the police, for a place in a police van and then for it to move. But she was lucky. Two women, including her buddy, were handcuffed behind and given the space at the back with only benches and bars and nothing to hold on to when it lurched or turned as she knew it always did. She had a seat amongst police, where the temperature might have been a degree or two higher, and her hands were free. Nonetheless her shivering jolted her with a rhythm that seemed to go unnoticed, and she didn't seem to be able to stop. No, the other two were told eventually, there were no blankets. Sometimes a cell was something to long for, especially if Warwickshire had that new vegan and gluten-free lasagne that was relatively enjoyable. By the time the van drove off to Nuneaton police station, around thirty bees were under arrest, but that left plenty more. Maybe some of them were locked on to tankers and maybe a few other tankers had flat tyres now. It couldn't all be for nothing, even though in her own case she'd only lasted five minutes on site before being drenched and knocked about as if the goal was to hurt as well as scare. And called a "fucking cunt".

Once at the station, arresting officers tended to relax in anticipation of the handover, and she counted on kindness and warmth from the custody sergeant. Her sodden coat and waterlogged boots were bundled into plastic but a concerned female brought her the usual grey sweatshirt and joggers, apologising that they were XL, and took her off to change. In the cell she had to remember, in view of the camera, to pull the waistband into a tube to hold whenever she stood. When she shed a few unexpected tears she acknowledged the shock, but doubted whether it qualified as trauma in the context of the suffering and death of those in the Global South who'd done least to create the climate crisis. Without a book she had to rely on talking, in their absence, to those she loved. And to God, in her own meditative Quaker way. Normally she danced a little, and did a few of the exercises she used to teach the kids as warm-ups before Games lessons, but the enormous joggers didn't encourage movement. And although cells were the only environments in which her singing voice sounded almost lovely, she couldn't find it, not a voice that held together. For the first time in more than a dozen arrests, she believed that if she closed her eyes she might actually sleep.

She wasn't charged, just bailed – no returning to the depot – and released under investigation into a bitter wind. Others waiting outside lent her a coat, gave her a hat and gloves. Someone would buy her train ticket home, and at the safe house the *Queen Mother* would serve hot food and drinks to each bee who arrived through the night. These were wonderful humans and some of them would go to prison but she wasn't sure she could do this again, any of it, and that made her feel feeble as well as old, and still over-sensitive after all these years – even though she told herself she'd done her best and that was way, way more than she'd imagined possible. All that mattered was stopping the madness that was everyday and utterly normal.

Sit for Climate

Sleek and red, the car at the lights
is the trophy kind,
a big cat tamed.
Sitting cross-legged behind my placard
I pay it no attention
until it snarls.
"Burn it!"
is the commentary I miss,
safe in my silence,
a smile-free zone.
But I hear the reprise,
the acid grind that tears like rage
or pain.
Oblivious to the message,
I guess at a problem,
some kind of failure.
And when I'm told,
I suppose I was right.

story written in June 2022

To the rescue: a grandma's tale

In a downmarket flat in a comfortable English town there lived a shy grandma. She lived with the guilt of breaking her children's hearts and she didn't suppose it would ever ease. But now that she had grandbabies she was determined to give them all the love and fun and care her slightly creaky body allowed. She sang to them, "You are my sunshine, my only sunshine," in a world where the darkness gathered thick around her. There was so much cruelty and injustice, and such helpless dependence on the fossil fuels set to end life on earth, that the tablets Grandma took weren't always enough. And there were times when fear for the future of the grandchildren she adored with a fervent, close-to-tears passion was overwhelming. If she hadn't already been willing to sit in the road, glue her hand to a bank window, or put her arm through a metal tube to block an oil depot or printing press just to push for the change the climate scientists cried out for, she would have joined the Rebellion when the first grandbaby slept in her arms. She'd been doing all that anyway, for the other children, the most vulnerable and furthest away. Now it was the least a grandma could do for three well-loved white children who lacked nothing except the prospect of the kind of life she'd once taken for granted.

But when she was with them, or their parents, it was a case of let's pretend, of being funny, acting up, dinosaurs and cuddles. The truth was too dark to allow in. All she really shared with their mums and dads was the arrests, court cases and personal stories of activists she admired. Not the reality. Not the details of the IPCC Reports or the Chatham House risk assessment, not the news of Thwaites Glacier… Like the BBC and most of the press, she kept shtum, because the real news was too horrifying to share with the children she'd brought into a world she hadn't known would die so fast.

She thought a lot about dying, which was cowardly because it was the biggest opt out of all. One thing, though, she was sure of: she would die for her grandchildren. No question. If that was all she had to do to save them, how simple everything would become. No hesitation. Wouldn't all the world's grandmothers do the same? Remembering being a young mum, and thinking about the sacrificial devotion of that new love, she reflected that parents dying for their children was a bit counter-productive, and that dying for her husband, whom she loved and who suffered as he aged, would simply increase his pain. But for a grandma, it made total sense. It would be the gift that kept on giving – if only it gave them life. And her darling partner would understand, as he mourned, because he understood the love as well as the science.

In stories love was magic and overcame evil. There were arcs and resolutions, and stirring courage. That was why Grandma had always loved stories much, much more than life, and needed to write her own. The alternative reality she created in her novels was a kind of redemption. In the books where she didn't feature she was her best self. But they weren't enough. They left the world unchanged and the earth on fire. And the only beauty that moved her was achingly sad, like the stories she loved best, like the innocence of the babies she couldn't protect from a world that would steal their laughter.

If this was a story, Grandma could fight off the lions that were about to attack her babies – but since she was vegan, would never fly again and signed petitions against trophy hunting, that wouldn't be the best climax. She could swim against wild water to rescue them from drowning. After all, they were so light that the three of them could ride on her back as she thrashed about, wishing she hadn't let hair loss and wigs keep her away from water for about four decades. So she was left with a fire that claimed her once she'd carried the grandbabies to safety. But that was too close to the real life narrative the media shunned. Birds were already falling from the sky and cattle carcases littering deserts. The present was frightening enough, and the future defied imagination.

Baddies added a frisson to her eldest grandson's play. "Let's not kill them," she'd recently deflected. "Let's turn them into goodies instead!" Only they were the smooth kind that wore suits, flew private jets and kept government and media under their oily thumbs. No matter how many times she protested, or was arrested, she couldn't defeat them, not with magic or even with love. Being the tragic heroine she'd identified with as a teenager was pointless if she couldn't save the grandchildren. And the planet too.

"Trusst in me," hissed the snake that ran Shell as he trailed greenwash around the earth. "Despair and die!" cried the White Witch, with Aslan under her knife. "Give up, it's hopeless," said the goblin clawing at Grandma's brain. The climate crisis is overstated, agreed nearly half the participants in the You Gov survey, before (and after) booking post-pandemic flights. "I serve the truth," whispered Grandma in the darkness when no one heard. She'd become obsessive, fanatical, extreme. And when she said goodbye to her grandchildren, she left the fun behind. "To conquer death," sang the Jesus of Superstar, "you only have to die." It wasn't the death that was the problem, she'd explained to the profound young philosopher who wasn't sure extinction would be such a bad thing. It was the dying: the suffering, the expectation, the chaos and terror and multi-sensory CGI drama. And the loss that already made the beauty acute.

If this was a story, the tears would be joyful, the ending exquisite, emotion rising and swelling above sentiment and absorbed down deep. Like the child she used to be, who imagined hunger striking until the killing stopped, she'd be the hero, alive or dead. But it was real, and all it had in common with the stories was the love. The narrative was suppressed, and what broke through to the light was jagged, torn, threadbare at times. People like Grandma were troublemakers, or words her mother didn't even know. They were enemies of the state and people. And all the love that bound them was redacted, lest anyone glimpsed its brightness and felt its power.

So it wasn't like the dark night when the ogre looked down on her grandbabies in their cots and licked its lips at three tasty snacks, but Grandma blocked the way, called herself a three-course meal and offered herself on a plate if it only let the babies dream on (a far, far better thing than she had ever done). There was no way but the hard way, the scorned way, the way that led regardless to the final ending. The only path worth taking, whatever the destination.

Better keep on keeping on.

poem written in June 2022

On Fathers' Day

I used to think his hands were beautiful
because of the way he drew,
and the pen strokes that formed the poems
like that Book of Hours without the gold.
The hands of a bullied boarder longing to be held,
of an evacuee
woken to the touch of grasses under quiet skies,
they led me into light and shade
and felt like happiness.
When mine grew textures, he took them still,
sensing the loss he carried too.
I knew by then how business sold and soiled the plans
on his city drawing board,
and how he clasped sadness
together with love
in a grip tighter than prayer.
And when his hand lay still and cool on a hospital sheet
and my mother couldn't let it go,
I felt it still, all of it,
the sadness, love, the light and shade
the longing and belonging,
the living out of hold.
I can still see his hands.

poem written in a courtroom, June 2022

Empowered

Courtrooms have lost their power
to intimidate,
to shrivel my voice
and take me back to schoolgirl fear
of detentions I never earned.
Only the coat of arms
casts pomp's sheen
on drab matte space,
an office less than functional.
The prosecutor speaks her lines
as if we're meant to understand
she didn't really write the play.
There's another script
littered with words like lies,
corruption and abuse
but it's banned, a no-go area,
a show-stopper,
a secret the public needn't know –
like the Code Red for humanity,
the prospect of extinction,
dead and dying children,
birds softly crashing
through searing blue
to raw baked earth.

Courtrooms have lost their power
to reduce me.
I'll take the stand, and only cry
for truth.

short story finished on my 66th birthday, July 2022

Back to the Future

There were a lot of dinosaurs in Sam's room, and nearly as many in Lola's. They had dinosaurs on their pyjamas, and their backpacks for school. But all these dinosaurs were small, and some of them were yellow, pink or mauve. That made them cute, especially if they were fluffy and meant to be cuddled.

"We'll never see a real dinosaur, Lola," Sam told his sister. "They're extinct."

Lola didn't understand that word but she was quite pleased anyway, because the pretend T. Rex at the zoo was enormous and made a horrible roar. And she only realised it wasn't real when Sam laughed at it and it didn't chase him.

Then one night Lola opened her eyes on the darkness and felt wide-awake. A diplodocus was leaning over her bed. It was so big that only its neck and head were in her room. When Lola looked out of the window, in case it would be a good idea to jump out, she saw that the rest of the diplodocus was outside. It was filling the road and making the trees and houses look smaller than usual. Meanwhile its giant face was close to hers in her bedroom.

That was when Sam appeared, climbed over the dinosaur's neck as if it was a fallen tree in a forest, and reminded Lola that the diplodocus was vegetarian. Which was good because otherwise it might eat their favourite cat, Buzz, who belonged to their favourite neighbours.

"If it was real," Sam said, "it would smell like a swamp and its breath would be stinky."

"Oh," said Lola, pinching her nose.

Sam decided to touch the stretch of neck that rested on Lola's rug just to show her he wasn't afraid. But no matter how close his hand came to its skin, he didn't feel anything at all. No scales and no bumps. His hand seemed to pass right through.

The dinosaur whispered but that sounded like distant thunder: "I haven't been alive for billions of years."

"That's what extinct means, Lola," Sam explained.

"But I've come back for a reason," added the diplodocus.

"To take us back in time?" suggested Sam, hopefully, because that was exciting in films.

The dinosaur shook its giant head. It seemed to be fading away, like a playground bruise but a hundred times faster.

"Don't go!" cried Lola, raising her arms as if she wanted a hug.

At that moment Sam and Lola heard footsteps. Their visitor must have heard too because it had disappeared completely. And in the morning, when they looked all around the garden, they couldn't find a single massive footprint anywhere.

"It'll come back," Sam told Lola at bedtime, when he kissed her goodnight.

"Why?" That was Lola's favourite question.

"Why not?" said Sam. But he did wonder whether the diplodocus had other children to visit too.

Lola and Sam were invited as usual to their neighbours' house the next Friday after school. That was what Daddy called a tradition, and nearly as exciting as Christmas, partly because Rajan and Ruth were as kind as pretend-grandparents and partly because of Buzz, who loved to walk with them, softly and slowly, his long tail stroking their legs.

"Buzz isn't very well, though," Mummy told them as they crossed the road. "He may be asleep."

"Oh," said Lola.

In fact Buzz lay on the sofa with his legs tucked in, like a supersoft cushion. Rajan said they needn't worry about waking him and it was all right to stroke him gently. The warm, round cushion moved up and down as Buzz breathed, silently and not very often.

"We may not have Buzz much longer," Ruth explained. "He's been poorly for a while but we didn't want to worry you. He's getting old and tired."

"Like us," added Rajan.

While Lola helped ice some biscuits Rajan had baked for them, Sam stayed with Buzz on the sofa and told him a story he'd never made up before, about a dinosaur that was friendly and magic and wouldn't eat him because it probably preferred broccoli. And peas – millions and millions of peas, a lorry load tipped down its throat by a JCB.

Buzz didn't stir all the time they were there, except for the small rise and fall of his breathing. When they left, for the first time ever he didn't walk them back over the road with his tail silkily tickling their legs.

"Is Buzz going to die?" Sam asked Mummy at bedtime.

"Yes, I think he will, sometime soon," Mummy said. "Everyone dies in the end."

"Even me and Lola?"

"You won't be old for a very, very long time," Mummy told him, and kissed his forehead. "So long I can't imagine what the world will be like by then."

Sam thought she sounded sad and he hadn't meant to upset her so he said, "Not to worry," like Grandad did when something got broken by mistake, or paint spilled in the wrong places.

Sometimes nothing happens for a while but you know it will. Lola dreamed every night that Buzz felt cold and hard because his heart had stopped. So it was no surprise when Rajan and Ruth invited them round to see Buzz's grave in a shady corner under their magnolia tree. Being there made Lola cry a little.

"We've collected some pebbles," said Ruth. "Would you arrange them in a heart while we see to some chocolate brownies?"

Sam and Lola did that carefully without arguing, and when they'd finished, they just stood there quietly, held hands and closed their eyes because they'd seen a funeral on TV. The garden was quiet except for the birdsong and Lola sniffing, so neither of them expected to open their eyes and find the diplodocus filling it. The outline of its huge body was misty, as if it was melting in the sun. Lola and Sam smiled at each other, and raised their joined hands so that they touched it. Or rather, passed right through it.

"Are you a ghost?" asked Sam.

The dinosaur's skin began to fade so fast that the garden was strung with gigantic bones, all of them connected and moving as one.

"It's a skel-e-ton," said Lola, one syllable at a time because that word was hard to say.

"Like the one in the museum!"

But they could see these bones were not as rocky. The skeleton felt no firmer than air. It didn't rattle and the feet made no sound on the grass. Sam nearly said he didn't want Buzz to turn into a skeleton too but he guessed Buzz would never know.

"What's it like being dead?" asked Lola.

Sam gave her a disapproving look.

"I've had plenty of time to get used to it!" cried the diplodocus, and the children supposed the rumbling, gurgling noise in their heads was a laugh.

"I didn't know dinosaurs were jokers," said Sam.

"Not so you'd notice," it admitted. The bones in its chest stopped shaking. "But seriously, dying is fine if the time is right and you're ready. It's just part of the circle of life."

To their astonishment the diplodocus began to sing that chorus – loudly, but not very well. Lola would have covered her ears but she didn't want to be rude.

"Children aren't," she said. "Ready, I mean."

The diplodocus shook its skeleton head, and just as Rajan called out of an open window, its bones disconnected and gathered in a pile beside Buzz's grave. Sam and Lola were about to bury them too when the sun grew so bright and the bones so white that for a moment the children were dazzled.

And then the bones had gone. Magnolia petals gathered softly where they had been. And on the bright earth where they'd shaped a heart, the pebbles were drifting, making a word. L-I-V-I-N-G. Sam started to sound it out. But no... The first 'I' wasn't straight any more. It rounded into an 'O' before the heart curved back in place. Now everything was still.

Through the open window they could smell the brownies, so Sam and Lola ran inside.

After that, Lola and Sam still visited their favourite neighbours to make sure they weren't sad without Buzz. Soon the magnolia flowers browned and mushed away but by summertime the jasmine on their back wall had opened out its little spiky petals to breathe all over the garden. Lola laughed when Ruth pretended to swoon because the scent was so dreamy. When Lola pretended too, she was so good at swooning that Ruth had to catch her.

Because Rajan had stopped cutting the grass in the middle of their garden, it was a wildflower meadow buzzing with bees and decorated with butterflies.

"So much life!" cried Rajan. "Don't you love it?"

"Yes!" cried Lola. She pictured the diplodocus smiling.

"Loving!" cried Sam, looking at Lola and back towards Buzz's grave. He would have felt embarrassed to shout that out in the school playground but here the word just settled like a bird on a branch. "Lola, that was it. The word!"

It was the only word he recognised on a painted sign lying in the sun. Lola opened her mouth and nodded as if she'd known that all along. Rajan laid his hand on Ruth's shoulder.

"You've got that right," he said.

Towards the end of the summer term the air was so hot that the teachers had to ban football in the playground. Sam felt sticky and a bit cross as July grew fierce and lessons felt longer and harder. One Friday, when a fresh breeze helped everyone feel a bit more alive, Lola sat sleepily in the shade of the PE shed, wondering where her brother was. Sometimes she missed him.

Lola was imagining the diplodocus, which made her smile. She wondered whether Sam was remembering too. So at first, when she squinted through sunlight at dinosaur back legs and a dinosaur backside rising up taller than a castle ahead of her, she just yawned. That was before she heard a voice: "Jump up!"

Lola didn't ask how, without a very long ladder. She didn't have to, because the diplodocus caught her up, with its bendy neck wrapped around her, and dropped her in place. She didn't seem to need a saddle or reins and she felt quite safe, as if she fitted.

"Sam!" she called, and found him landing next to her, crying, "Whoah!"

The children could see that the diplodocus had a bus-sized placard hanging and swinging from its neck but they couldn't read it. Some of the older children could, though, because they cheered. From all around the playground children were being scooped up and whisked through the air. Dozens of them were gathering on the dinosaur's back – as if it was a bus and they were ready for a magical school trip. And some of them didn't wear Sam and Lola's uniform. He realised they were being collected from the other side of the world, and they looked hungry, frightened or sad – until they laughed.

"Look!" cried Sam. "Mrs Grubb's on the roof!"

The head teacher and all her staff were up where the view was best. The last few were scaling the fire escape. But none of them looked scared. They were waving wildly and giving thumbs-up to the giant placard.

As the diplodocus swung its neck right round Sam caught a glimpse of big clumsy letters that might have been written in mud.

"FRIDAYS FOR something," he said. Not fun or football.

"Who knew dinosaurs couldn't spell?" chuckled Mrs Grubb.

And then, as if time had suddenly run right out on a computer game, or the diplodocus had pulled out a plug with its tail, the dinosaur vanished – leaving children tumbling and spinning safely onto grass. Teachers and teaching assistants were scuttling down the fire escape. Then for a moment the only sound was the cooling breeze. It was so quiet that Sam thought he could hear everything grow. Well, not the teachers; they'd stopped.

With fat coloured chalks, passed from one hand to another, everyone who could write wrote a message at their feet, or on the wall behind them. The younger children like Lola made criss-cross kisses. The teachers wrote some long words. Sam took care when it was his turn because he didn't want Mrs Grubb to say dinosaurs weren't the only ones that couldn't spell.

SAVE LIFE, he wrote, and drew a tree with a bird up in its branches. He thought about the children from faraway who might not have a home any more.

Wiping the sweat dripping under his cap, Sam told Lola what the words said.

"That's why the diplodocus came," he said.

"I know," said Lola.

At home time, Mum said all the parents had been sent a text from Mrs Grubb.

"That's good. The school is going to support Fridays for Future from now on."

Ah, thought Sam, FUTURE! It was funny that it took a diplodocus from the past to teach humans to take care of that.

"The thing is," said Lola, "the future starts with now," and she opened her arms to the world.

poem written in July 2022,
inspired by a photograph discovered on Twitter

Black and white

He's gagged,
clasped supplicant's hands bound
as if by scoring wire.
But what's torn from his wrists
drips black,
like the message on his bright white vest,
like the spill oozing slick from
his crucified head,
like the melting shine of his skin.
He's Paralympian shoulders,
and biceps that power the wheels,
but the chest that reads
LIFE BEFORE PROFIT
caves, beaten.
Like the Earth he holds, painted to weep oil,
he cries unheard,
a tableau with no voice,
a slave to hot white greed,
a prisoner tortured
by great white hope
thrown from a podium like cake
iced and ribboned for the camera
but crumbling and too stale for birds.
Nameless, he lifts eyes to God,
is fire,
longs for rain,
runs with poison.
I ache, and save, then scroll on down.
And far away
he's gone.

short story written in July 2022

Breaking Out

Nico was a step behind his mum, dodging the swirl of her hippy skirt like a cat on the shoreline avoiding a wave. It was meant to be a tour but his eyes seemed drawn to the parched earth and the grass fading to white. Turning, his mum noticed and said, "Oh look, Nico, what a lovely natural sandpit." The girl dangling thin bare legs from the pale log above it cast a loud "Hello!" like a challenge in his direction. His mum wouldn't expect him to answer but the mentor guiding them around might wonder why he pretended he hadn't heard. Nico supposed his mum had told them about his issues. She probably hoped this place would mend him.

He hadn't pointed out to her in the car that none of this was his idea. He was used to hating school and at least he knew where to hide and how. "I don't know anyone who's home-schooled," he'd objected, as if he had friends to miss. It was because of the divorce. Arguing about what was best for Nico animated both his parents, even by email. He'd caught a glimpse of the long one from his father signed off with: *I can't let you sacrifice Nico to your Earth Mother fantasy.*

The mentor, who had a long curly black beard and shiny brown scalp, pointed out the circle of logs around soft, dark ash.

"For the Children's Fire," he said, giving that capitals and lifting it into a question as if it had a special meaning he hoped they understood. "We start and finish here every day. It's a time of reflection and gratitude – and song, of course."

Nico could just smell the trace of smoke stirred by breeze. He liked flames but not the bitterness in his mouth. His mother was smiling non-stop and using words like lovely, wonderful and amazing but he hadn't spoken since confirming his name.

They were heading for a large pond topped with something sludgy and yellow that looked like his mum's gram flour batter left to rot. All around it plants erupted, tall as him and dense as a hedge. Nico trailed the stick he'd picked up through the ochre coating down into brown water where a fat, black beetle swam. It didn't look as if it was afraid of anything. Its legs started to cling tentatively to the end of his stick before it swam away in a scrambling kind of hurry.

The pond looked smelly but it wasn't. Like him! Or maybe he was, in this kind of heat which his mum called insane. He'd check his armpits when no one was looking. All the girls here were flowery with hair that blew in the breeze and he wouldn't want them to see him sniffing where the cotton was dark.

"And this," said the bearded mentor, "is the allotment. It's running us ragged at the moment but it means lunch grows fifty metres from the kitchen."

Nico thought the allotment looked ragged too but he wouldn't mind it keeping him busy.

"Nico's a vegan," his mum announced, "who doesn't like vegetables!"

He frowned. That was what they called misinformation because he liked at least six, and fruits that didn't pack surprise pips. Apparently he wouldn't be the only vegan at Chrysalis Learning, which made his mum very happy for someone who couldn't give up chicken or lamb.

Ahead of them was a small wooden building with solar panels on the roof. Out in front of it was a long table with boxes stored underneath. But what were the children touching? He could see it was flat and soft, and a red kind of brown.

"Although our menu is meat-free," their guide said, "roadkill is a learning opportunity. This is one of our dads, who hit a deer on the road the other night. Look how small the skull is, Nico."

It was white but someone must have scrubbed the blood and flesh away. His fingers knew how hard it was so they didn't need to touch the bone. But his hand reached for the deerskin and found it so warm it felt alive.

"My dad had to go on a driving course when he was careless," said Nico, "and drunk."

"Oh Nico, no one meant to run over the deer," said his mum.

He wondered whether she'd already told the adults here that he was sensitive. People who didn't mind animals being killed for burgers and bacon weren't. They didn't care that cows could cry and pigs were as clever and sensitive as dogs. If he found a dead deer he'd bury it even if it took all day to dig a hole big enough to cover the antlers and he'd say something like, "Peace be with you" like they did at his father's old-fashioned church.

The classrooms had blackboards like the old days, and no computers. Lots of artwork hung around the walls and windows, swinging brightly in the light and breeze. Nico was no good at any of that. Colours always turned to mud when he mixed them.

With a class of thirty you could sit at the back and pretend you were just a ghost but this would be different. He could tell the tour had come to an end, and looking at the copse around one side he realised how much he wanted to step inside where the colours were darker.

"Well, I'm blown away," said his mum. "Thank you so much, Arun."

She was the tallest woman he knew and his dad called her an amazon without the offers which – he'd had to explain – meant she was robust and her hair was wild. She was the reason some kids in Y7 told him to duck when he walked through a door. But everything blew her away: fabric, ceramics and glass; art galleries, David Bowie and Nina Simone; roses with scent; other people's babies. His father said it was tiring.

She didn't say anything when Nico wandered off to the trees. It would give her a chance to talk about him. But in the little wood someone had marked out tiny rooms like the floor plans of houses for sale, which made him feel like he was trespassing.

"What do you think, Nico?" he asked himself, before his mother could. He knew she'd add, "Don't say you don't know." Not knowing was safe except about climate change. That was insanely dangerous and yoga wouldn't fix it. Neither would this place and that was the trouble.

The earth under his feet was hard enough to scratch like glass. In Pakistan birds were falling from the sky and that wasn't roadkill, it was coalkill. Oilkill. But no one in Bedfordshire seemed to care and everyone called the weather fantastic even though really that meant extraordinary and remarkable, and odd like him. Not fun to celebrate.

Even the shade was baked. The children's voices were muted now because lessons were starting under a canopy or indoors. His mother was striding towards him, her skirt swelling around her legs.

"Hey!" she said as he emerged. "We have a couple of trial days next week before term ends. Then you could start in September if you liked it. As if anyone could not like it. I mean… heaven or what?"

His dad was the religious one now but the church was so stony grey. Nico didn't answer but followed her towards the car his parents were fighting over. Neither of them liked it when he said electric wasn't the answer because of the particulates and the minerals for the batteries that were mined by children.

"What would I do on the other three days?" he asked as he fastened his seat belt. The metal around them was hot enough to fry a tomato and the air it trapped was sickly sweet.

"Lessons – you, me and the internet. Trips to London for art galleries and museums. Baking – when the heatwave ends – and an instrument maybe, if you like. Our own curriculum."

"She likes to think she's radical," his father said. Over Dad's body, he told her in his head, remembering the deer that really was just skin and bone. But she wouldn't let him go to Parliament Square with Fridays for Future because "It would just cause so much trouble, love."

"What about exams?" he asked as the car glided down the hill and everything stretched out golden around them.

"Yes, well, you know your father thinks you need those."

No jobs on a dead planet. Nico would tell him that one day when the words were firm.

"But not if they stress you," his mum added. "No need to plan that far ahead."

For a while, along lanes that bent and narrowed and sometimes broke into dust, she sang under her breath to save talking and Nico tried to think like a scientist looking at data and measuring it. He'd be alone at Chrysalis Learning and he'd never be a butterfly like the girls in their prints, so although it was all the difference in the world it was also all the same.

But was it fair to be somewhere beautiful that cost money when other kids were in their uniform at the factory farm with no trees to make shadows and voices like percussion clashing? That might be a poem. Dark things were, especially if they were sad and lonely. But lockdown had been safe, apart from the arguments, and he missed it in a way. This might be second best. Maybe they'd teach him how to build a shelter in a forest, and forage without eating the wrong mushrooms. They called that resilience, but not the kind his dad had in mind which meant joining in, fitting, trying harder to be normal.

"I liked the taste of the air," he said.

Sometimes he nearly made her laugh which he didn't really mind. At the end of her smile she nodded, and touched his bare arm.

"We'll be all right," she said.

poem written in August 2022 after a dream

Last Gasp

It begins between *Jaws* and *Titanic*
and water that surges and hurls
but when I find the air through spray
I see, inside a captive, thrashing whale,
a child, hair buffeted and streaming
in a Leonardo womb,
unbirthed, eyes wide, stillborn.
It's a while before I understand, as shallows gape,
the other death,
so deep is it into blinding darkness
on an invaded and alien shore.

Awake only to awe
I feel power trickle helpless into night.

children's story first published by Magic Oxygen, 2017

The Dragons' Daughter

The dragon's nest was lined with leaves and feathers. It was cosy, but the child grew fast. Soon she could crawl over the top. She had no idea how high up the mountain the dragons had built her nest, or why. There was a long, long way to fall with no wings. So the dragons took turns to guard her. One would stay close enough to tickle her with warm dragon breath. The other flew overhead, watching out for danger with round green eyes.

When the sun was fierce, her dragon parents lifted one wing each, till they joined. Then the child had her own scaly green tent to keep her cool. But soon she was walking. It was harder to keep her safe and harder to understand her talk. The dragons loved her, but she puzzled them. They didn't always know how to make her happy. Dragon's milk was not enough for her now, but how should they feed her?

That summer, Spell the mother dragon had an idea. She swooped down at night to snatch the corn from the fields. She flew home with a golden mouthful between her teeth. Then Cloud the father dragon ground it between big flat rocks, until it was flour. Now they needed water to mix, but water was a problem. Dragons took cover when it rained. They never, ever splashed in rocky pools like the child. Her dragon parents didn't want to be splashed, thank you. But now she splashed the dough. Then she mixed it with her little fingers.

Baking was never a problem for dragons. They just had to roar on wood and it blazed. The bread soon crisped in a little stony oven. It was flat but the child seemed to like it. She filled two slices with berries she picked herself, standing on Cloud's head.

While she slept, the father dragon breathed gently down on the nest. He took care not to burn the child's small brown ears or singe her dark, fluffy hair. He breathed just enough to keep her warm.

When Spell returned, she said the town below was quiet. The weather was too hot for dragon-sighting trips up the mountain.

"The humans are at the beach," she said.

Cloud shuddered at the thought of seawater and waves.

"The child needs a new nest," Spell told him.

"The child needs many things we can't give her," said Cloud. He shook his head and tail.

"She needs a name," said Spell, as the child stirred.

Spell looked at the sleeping child's soft brown skin, so different from their tough green dragon scales. Just at that moment, the child woke and Spell winked at her.

"She's smooth," said the mother dragon.

So Smooth became her name.

*

Smooth helped to build the new nest. She found flowers to thread it with colour and scent. She chose pretty pebbles from around the rock pools. Her parents polished them with dragon flame. Then they slotted them in between the twigs and leaves so that they sparkled in sunlight.

As Smooth grew, she learned to climb. There were things she could do that dragons never did. She taught herself to float in the mountain pools, and ride the mountain streams. But Smooth loved her dragon parents and she wanted to be just like them. She just didn't know how.

However hard she blew out of her snub brown nose, no fire flamed and no smoke curled. It made the dragons laugh their hissy, sizzling laughs. Smooth tried to laugh like that, but her chuckle was watery, not warm.

Smooth was sure she could fly. But nothing happened when she flapped her smooth brown wings. Her bare feet only lifted a moment and landed again.

"No flying, Smooth!" cried Spell.

"Promise not to try!" Cloud told her.

They could see she was ready for some new excitement. So Spell and Cloud gave her sky rides every day.

"Up you get!" Cloud would tell her, crouching on all fours and giving her a bright green wink.

Then Smooth would clamber onto his back and hold on tightly. Meanwhile Spell flew below, ready to catch her if she cried, "Look! No hands!" and tumbled down. Smooth was such a daring child. Soon she was asking for night rides – beneath the moon, when the wind was wild.

She wasn't afraid of darkness, not even in the cool cave. Cloud wouldn't go inside that, because it dripped without warning and made him jump and shiver.

She wasn't afraid to look down at the world of people, because people were too small to see. She couldn't begin to imagine what a human would look like. But she was sure they couldn't be half as brave as dragons, or as funny.

Her dragon parents thought she understood about fire. But that winter, when it was icy on the mountain, she gave them a fright. Cloud felt the cold, and his scaly snout was turning blue. Suddenly he sneezed – all over a bush. At once it flamed and smoked, so Cloud sat on it, just enough to warm through.

Waking at the sound of the sneeze, the child didn't see the flames underneath his scaly dragon bottom. She only saw the smile on his dragon face. She ran to join him in his big dragon's nest!

"No!" cried Spell.

"Aaaagh!" cried the child as she hit a wall of heat.

Now her grass dress was flecked with crispy black. Her skin was still brown and smooth, but rather sore.

That night as she slept, the dragons felt afraid for their fearless daughter.

"We should take her back," said Cloud, "like the other babies."

"She isn't like the others," Spell told him, as if he didn't know.

Smooth wasn't the only baby they'd rescued, beating their wings through fire the way only dragons can. They'd found human homes for the others, but Smooth was the one they'd kept. Now they couldn't imagine life without her.

*

Smooth began to ask questions.

"Why can't I fly?" she asked. Or, "Why can't I breathe fire?"

The only answer her dragon parents ever gave her was, "One day you'll understand."

Whenever they spotted a dragon-sighting bus winding its way up the mountain, they cried, "Hide, Smooth, quickly!"

Cloud and Spell were good at hiding, right at the tops of the tallest trees. Their wings pretended to be leaves and their bodies blended into the bumpiest, knottiest trunks. As long as they didn't cough any flames, the dragon-hunters never spotted them. They all had their eyes on the skies. And Cloud and Spell had their eyes on them.

It was different for Smooth. She couldn't climb fast or high enough. So she always had to hide under leaves in the darkest, coldest corner of the drippy cave. And she'd had enough of it.

"Why must I hide when the bus comes?" she asked. "What are people like?"

"They're not safe," said Cloud.

"Or tasty," said Spell, and showed her teeth as she winked.

The next time the tour bus started up the mountain, the dragons roared the alarm. Before they flew to the treetops they nudged Smooth into the cave with their wings. Smooth was cold and alone. And besides, she wanted to see these people. She wanted to find out for herself how many legs they had. She wanted them to know she wasn't afraid.

Under the leafy blanket Smooth heard voices. Through the cave they echoed and filled her head.

"Move on, everyone," she heard. "Dragons don't like caves that drip."

A beam of light that wasn't sunshine circled Smooth. It dazzled her so she couldn't see the humans at the entrance to the cave.

"Dragons are afraid of water," said the guide, as if everyone knew that.

Smooth heard a rude giggle. It made her cross. Pushing her way free of the leaves, she stood tall.

"I'm NOT!" she said.

"It's a child!" she heard.

Smooth looked around because she had no idea what a child might be.

"Here, my dear," she heard. "I have a tasty treat for you. Come and get it."

Smooth was curious, and hungry too. Unafraid, she ran towards the light. Suddenly the air stirred with the flapping of dragon wings. The people screamed as Cloud and Spell circled their heads. The dragons breathed down enough fire to turn the human ears very red. Spell's roar filled every one of those ears, and the cave too.

Screaming, the people ran out of the darkness towards the tour bus. Smooth chuckled at all the humans scampering in a panic. They fell over each other as they bundled into the coach on wheels. Above it, her dragon parents shrouded them with smoke.

Smooth drew closer to the tour bus because she wanted a clearer view of the human faces through the windows. Still she had no fear – until a human arm grabbed her and pulled her in. That moment the bus moved off.

"Don't worry, dear," said one, as the bus wound its way down the mountain track. "You'll be fine now."

*

THWACK! A dragon wing beat against the bus. The air around it was wild with dragon roars. Spell's flaring dragon nostrils pressed against the window. With a fierce swing, a dragon tail knocked the bus from behind. The bus tilted as if it would fall like a tree in a storm. Brakes screeched. The human screams around her burst inside Smooth's head. But the bus turned the bend and rolled on, still upright.

Smooth saw Cloud shake his head at Spell. The dragon parents could only watch as Smooth was driven away from them, down towards the world of people.

And Smooth could only watch as they flew away.

"Did anyone get a photo?" she heard.

"Are you serious?" asked someone. "We're lucky to escape with our lives."

"I want my money back," said someone else. "No danger, you said. Dragons are shy, you said!"

"Quiet," Smooth heard. "You're scaring the child."

"I'm not scared," said Smooth, "and I'm not a child. Take me home." Then she remembered the manners her dragon parents had taught her. "Please."

"Where do you live?" asked a deep-voiced human with a hairy chin.

Smooth frowned. People were very silly. "Up there," she said, pointing.

"Where are your parents, dear?" asked a fleshy person with a flame-red mouth.

"Up there," said Smooth.

The humans looked at each other.

"Learning difficulties, Mr Highcastle?" muttered someone.

"She needs a bath," said the tall human with the hairy face, grabbing his nose.

"My goodness, child," said the red mouth, "is that dress made of grass?"

"Eek!" squealed someone as a large beetle crawled out of the dress Cloud had woven.

So Smooth ate the beetle. After that she had the back seat of the bus to herself.

It seemed like a long ride down to the town. As she stepped down from the bus, Smooth looked up to the pointed hat of a building with a tall tower, just in case Spell or Cloud was perched on top of it. But only pigeons gathered there. Smooth felt sad and alone.

"Where are we going?" she asked.

Back on the mountain, Cloud and Spell had nothing to say. They had no heart for soaring or roaring and they felt sure they would never wink again. Of course they'd always known a child could never really be a dragon. But could Smooth really learn to be a child?

*

The humans knew what Smooth needed. It was called boarding school. First she was washed and dried without any rain or sunshine. Instead of her grass dress she wore something called uniform. Onto her clean feet they tied hard and heavy shells they called boots.

The humans in uniform were called pupils, and the pupils who found it hard to sit or walk were called boys. Like Smooth, the boys would rather run and climb. But they didn't want her to play. They only looked at her as if they weren't sure what she could be. And the girls kept away, with their noses up.

The tall humans were teachers. They carried big sticks called canes but Smooth didn't know what they were for. Smooth lived a new life now, full of knives, forks and napkins. The newest pupil had a lot to learn.

At the boarding school Smooth learned to understand numbers and write her name. Soon she knew that balls were for beating until they flew, or catching when they tried to land. But music was best. It seemed to Smooth a kind of magic. In her first lesson she saw humans pluck watery bird notes from boxes with strings across a hole. The sounds were so beautiful that when she closed her eyes she was sure she was flying...

"Smooth!" snapped a teacher, beating his cane on the desk. "No dreaming!"

Smooth soon learned not to scowl, growl or bare her teeth even when she was angry. And sometimes that was hard. But the hardest lesson was the one she learned at bedtime on her very first night, and it was the mirror that taught her. Smooth had to be shown what a toothbrush was for and what to do with a comb. In the silvery glass she saw the truth. Not a dragon but a hairy child with wild, staring eyes. When she snarled, the child snarled back.

Smooth watched the tear trickle from her reflection's eye. But she felt it, slippery and cool on her own skin.

"I'm not a dragon," she murmured, "after all."

In the bedroom she looked at the crisp white sheet with no leaves, no jewels and no feathers. She wondered how she was meant to sleep. There was no breeze to burrow through her hair and make it flicker like dragon flame. Cloths called curtains shut out the moon. Stroking them, Smooth felt sure she'd seen them in her dreams, making a wall around her as she rocked...

"But I am the dragons' daughter," she whispered.

She would make them proud of her.

*

The humans all had their own names and the tallest had three: Headmaster, Mr Highcastle and Sir. The hair on his face was not a nest but a beard, and sometimes he scratched it. But the school didn't belong to him. The owner was a rich man called Lord Wishnomore, who was too important to visit. Smooth could tell Mr Highcastle was afraid of him. The Headmaster only had to hear the name of Lord Wishnomore and his head would wobble on his long skinny neck.

The other pupils all looked neater than Smooth. Mrs Highcastle was Matron so she inspected beds. And heads.

"Is this hair," she asked, looking round at the other children, "or an old nest?" Her mouth was always red but she never talked about treats any more.

"It's a disgrace!" she tutted, looking at Smooth's crumpled bed. "We'll have to call you Wrinkles."

Even after Matron cut and scrubbed her dirty, jagged nails, no one sat next to Smooth in class. Sometimes she looked up from her work to find someone staring as if she really did have wings and a tail.

One day at playtime she heard a question thrown at her from behind.

"Who taught you English," asked a girl with a shiny pony tail, "if your parents are dragons?"

The girl's name was Lavelle and she called Lord Wishnomore daddy. She seemed to think she was very special.

Smooth explained that dragons could speak any language they chose. "My father Cloud talks Italian when he cooks," she said. "My mother Spell likes to mutter Latin before she breathes her best infernos."

"What's an inferno?" squeaked Jack, the smallest boy in school. Jack's nose was always running but so were his eyes, behind his crooked glasses.

"A huge, wild, flaming, roaring blaze," Smooth told him. She showed him with her arms.

Jack's nose was so messy that Mr Highcastle shouted, "Boy! Handkerchief!" and waved his cane. Smooth stared at it. She imagined it ablaze in a very small inferno. She pictured the Headmaster dropping the flaming cane right on his foot, gasping and hopping. If only she was a dragon…

But she wasn't, so she lent Jack her hankie.

That night before bed, Lavelle was brushing her glossy hair when she stopped and looked at Smooth.

"Who cut your hair?"

"My parents," said Smooth, "with their claws."

Lavelle sighed. Then she asked another question, with a honey-sweet voice: "Why do you tell lies?"

Smooth could almost feel smoke tickling her ears and nostrils. She bared her teeth as a growl caught in her throat. Her burning eyes blazed at Lavelle, who screamed. Some children ran away.

Smooth saw the fear on Jack's pale face, and felt sorry. She gave him a friendly wink and he stopped sniffing.

"Oh dear, Wrinkles," said Lavelle, as Mr Highcastle marched towards them, holding his cane high the air. "You're in trouble now."

"Smooth!" yelled the Headmaster.

Smooth wasn't afraid. She turned to Lavelle with a cheeky grin, and winked.

*

Smooth wasn't caned. She was locked in a cupboard. It wasn't as dark as the cave and it didn't drip. There was paper on the shelves and chalk in boxes so she drew the mountain, and the dragons flying over it.

At bedtime Matron unlocked the door. But that night Smooth missed her dragon parents more than ever. She missed the stars she could almost reach on her moonlit rides. In the big, long bedroom all she could hear was the ticking of a clock. But even though it had a kind of face, it never winked. And sometimes in her dreams she looked up from a cot to see dragons bat the flames away...

Every morning when the post arrived, other pupils opened letters from parents, but there was never anything for Smooth.

"Can't your parents write?" asked Lavelle. She smiled at the others. "It must be hard to hold a pen with dragon claws."

Some of the children giggled but some of them didn't dare. Smooth had nothing to say, because nobody would believe her.

Then one morning Mr Highcastle had some news. Soon it would be Open Day. Lord and Lady Wishnomore would be special guests, but all the parents were invited. Smooth would like Cloud and Spell to know how quick her maths could be. She asked Mr Highcastle whether they'd had their invitation.

He smiled. "Where would we post it, Smooth?"

Smooth knew no one would venture as high up the mountain as her empty nest. "The post van could deliver it," she said, "to the cave."

Mr Highcastle nodded, and walked away with his black cloak floating behind him.

Day after day, Smooth felt a tangle of hope whenever the post arrived. But there was never a letter with Smooth Dragon on the envelope. Hadn't they found the invitation? Had Cloud and Spell forgotten all about her? Smooth went sadly to bed, listening to the other pupils whispering about seeing their parents the next day.

A sudden flare of flame broke through the gap in the curtains. The other children gasped. Smooth sprang out of bed. Her nostrils quivered at the smell of smoke, and she knew it wasn't the human kind that rose from the chimney.

Eagerly, Smooth looked for her dragon parents. There was no sign of them, not a swish of tail or the tip of a wing in flight! But holding the curtains apart, Smooth read the evening sky. The message was bright green on grey and the letters looped and joined, large and curly:

See you soon, Smooth.

The other children gathered behind Smooth, their mouths wide open like their eyes. As the sentence faded away, another one formed:

Love from your proud dragon parents.

A row of flame-red kisses decorated the sky.

*

Smooth woke next morning with a smile on her face. She looked in the mirror and winked. She scrubbed her face and brushed her hair. Cloud and Spell had never seen her looking so clean. She hoped they would recognise her!

The sky was clear and blue. Looking toward the mountains, Smooth could hardly wait. The other pupils were excited too, all of them except Jack. He was still in bed, facing the wall with the blanket up to his nose.

"What's wrong, Jack?" asked Smooth.

"My parents can't come," mumbled Jack. "They never come."

Smooth felt sorry for him but he'd be in trouble if he didn't get dressed quickly.

"When mine arrive," she told him, "I'm hoping for a ride. Maybe you'd like one too?"

Jack turned with rounded eyes. "On a dragon?"

Smooth nodded. Jack was the only one who believed her. He jumped out of bed and bounced, as if he was ready to fly himself.

"That's settled then," said Smooth. She thought a glide on Cloud's steady back would suit a first-timer. Not a whirling mid-air spin or two with daredevil Spell!

For the next hour or two Jack never left Smooth's side. They blew on their porridge together at breakfast and walked in step along the corridor. They watched from the same window. Then the Headmaster blew a whistle and each pupil sat at a desk with some numbers to add. "Heads down!" he shouted. It was a kind of show and the parents would soon be the audience.

Motor cars began to draw up outside. One was so huge and shiny that Smooth half-expected the King to step out. Lavelle sat up straight as a very smart couple walked into the hall. Mr Highcastle jumped, and put on the biggest smile Smooth had ever seen.

"Lord and Lady Wishnomore," he murmured, and bowed so low he nearly bent in half. "Smooth!" he snapped. "Head down please!"

Smooth was just about to turn back to her numbers when a familiar smell made her nostrils twitch. Looking up and out of the window, she saw two green shapes spread across the sky, wingtip to wingtip. Then one twisted, dived and flipped for the fun of it.

In the school hall no one moved. As Cloud and Spell flew closer by the second, little red flames circled their heads like petals. Jack opened his mouth and clapped his hands.

Leaping up, Smooth ran for the double doors onto the courtyard and opened them wide. Her dragon parents glided down to land. Smooth heard the clatter of claws on the polished wooden floor.

Smooth smiled. Spell winked. Cloud stood up on his back legs and bowed to Lord and Lady Wishnomore. But they leaned against the wall as if they might slide right down it and onto the floor.

Matron screamed and hid behind the curtains on the school stage. Mr Highcastle ran to the piano and crouched behind it. Lavelle shrieked and climbed on top of it. Now Jack couldn't help it; he laughed out loud.

Pressed between her dragon parents, Smooth was happy again. It had never felt so good to be loved.

"Smooth!" cried Cloud, carefully patting her head with one front foot. "Just look at you!"

*

Smooth smiled but it was different now. She had looked at herself. She felt her mouth quiver. She wanted to ask her dragon parents about her dreams. She needed to know about the cot wrapped in smoke and the dragon wings batting it away.

"You're a princess!" gasped Spell, and Jack cheered.

"But I'm not a dragon," she said.

Spell's scaly shoulders stiffened and her neck stretched up high. Her nostrils were wide and dark. "Who told you that?" she wanted to know.

Spell turned her head to look around the hall. At the sight of her swirly green eyes, everyone looked nervously away.

"Not me!" called a voice from behind the piano.

"Or me," came another, muffled by curtains.

"Never mind," said Cloud, calmly. "It's Open Day. We don't know what parents do."

"But we'd like to start with a riding lesson," said Spell. She looked at the piano. "If that's all right with the Headmaster?"

Mr Highcastle peered up from behind the piano. He looked around the hall, but Lord and Lady Wishnomore had vanished.

"By all means, please do, feel free!" the Headmaster squeaked.

Smooth reached out for Jack. She had to give him a foothold and a lift-up. Then he scrambled, wriggly with excitement, onto Cloud's powerful back. There were two shoulder blades he could hold like handles.

With the grace of a dancer Cloud took off, out across the courtyard and upward. The sound of Jack's breathless giggle filled the silent hall. Waving, Smooth climbed onto Spell. A moment later she was in the air again, remembering how it felt to ride the wind. Wild as a storm, Spell flashed, spun and zigzagged across the sky. Was it the best ride ever? Or had Smooth forgotten how good it felt to be free?

All too soon, the dragons turned back towards the school, dark and tiny below. Swooping down, they landed together.

"We're here to discuss our daughter's progress," Spell told the piano.

Mr Highcastle's hat appeared first, then his head, his beard and neck.

"Of course," he said. "May I offer you a cup of tea?"

Matron's head appeared between the curtains, her face very white.

"Cake?" she asked.

*

Smooth's dragon parents said no to tea. It was much too wet. But they liked the cake, once they'd roasted it crispy black. And they were very pleased with Smooth's work and her manners. She saw their pride when she stood to recite the eleven times table – perfectly.

"It sounds like magic!" cried Spell.

When she played the violin, their tails swayed as dreamily as their dragon heads. And Smooth could tell, from the way they smiled when they sniffed her, how much they liked her soapy smell.

Jack, who couldn't read or write yet, showed them everything he'd made. The dragons clapped his clay model of a bug and his painting of the sun. Jack seemed to like the feel of dragon skin and the warmth of dragon breath. His nose and eyes were quite dry. While Smooth read a story she'd written about a girl in a dragon's nest, Jack sat on a dragon lap. Still and rosy-cheeked, he listened with Cloud's tail curled around him.

If Smooth hadn't felt so peaceful, she might have wondered why Mr Highcastle looked so pleased with himself.

"Ahem," he coughed, bowing to the dragon parents. "May I invite you to step into the courtyard – for a private word?"

"Of course," said Cloud.

Smooth started to follow but the Headmaster told to her to take Jack for some more cake. So she watched her parents waddle outside, their two dragon tails curling up and linking behind them. Smooth took Jack's hand.

He loved the cake. In fact, his chin was coated in icing. But it was also wobbly now, as if the dragons would never come back.

"It's all right," she told him.

Smooth turned as the doors to the courtyard slammed shut. She heard the bolts rammed in hard. Something made her look up. There on the tiled rooftops she saw men. It was the caretaker and his team. But what were they holding?

From every roof around the courtyard, a steely rain fell down. Sharp darts pierced dragon skin. Spell breathed a burst of fire, but a second later her eyelids closed. Cloud groaned before his head slumped onto his chest. Like large green hedgehogs they were spiked now. Like hedgehogs they seemed ready to sleep for a very long time.

Smooth ran towards the courtyard where her dragon parents lay quite still. She rattled at the door handles. Jack let out a sob.

"Now!" cried a voice from a skylight window. Smooth saw Lord Wishnomore waving down like a signal.

An enormous net dropped down from the school roof and landed over Cloud and Spell.

*

By supper time all the other parents had left. Smooth had no appetite. She tried to listen for a dragon roar. Maybe they'd woken, and ripped the net apart with their great black claws? But Smooth couldn't sneak away to check. She was watched every moment by Lavelle, who wore a whistle round her neck.

"They're only dragons," said Lavelle. "They're not human. They're just a species, like rats."

Smooth bared her teeth and dropped her knife and fork on the table.

"No one's going to hurt them," said Lavelle. "Daddy says it's business. People will pay just to see them, or take a summer course in Dragon Studies."

Smooth's scowl was so dark Lavelle jumped. But what could Smooth do? It was all her fault. She should never have sent the letter! She should have left them alone to forget all about her.

Every time she saw Jack, he was whimpering and sniffing.

"Have they flown away?" he asked her at bedtime. Smooth couldn't lie. She only tried to comfort him by stroking his hot forehead.

In the mirror where she washed her face, she looked sad and very tired. But how could she sleep?

"You're so ungrateful," said Lavelle in the candlelit corridor. "Other parents pay to send their children here but your place is free. That's because you're just a penniless orphan. The least your so-called parents can do is earn Daddy's school some money."

The least I can do, thought Smooth, is set my parents free. Lying in her bed, she imagined the night sky lit by fire as they headed back to the mountain. If she could stay awake, maybe she could find a way to make it real.

It was long after midnight when Smooth tiptoed past the other beds. Then she stopped. Lavelle's beautiful hair was spread on her pillow. The whistle lay around her neck but she was fast asleep.

Smooth padded along to the bathroom. It was empty. On the landing she listened but there was nothing to hear. Down the wide staircase she crept without a creak.

Stopping as she turned the corner, she looked down to the courtyard, half-expecting to find it guarded. But it lay in darkness beneath the stars. Then the moon broke free of clouds overhead. By its pale light she could see the silver of water as the fountain whispered.

But no guards, no net and no dragons.

Smooth felt the bite of the night wind as it caught her nightdress. She must not be afraid. Wherever they were, she would find them – and a way to rescue them.

*

The clock struck two. Smooth had looked everywhere from the kitchens and cellars to the staff room. Now her eyes lifted to the night skies, as if she'd find a message winding between the stars: Safely home! Smooth told herself to keep thinking, but where else could they be?

Creeping into the gardens she heard a sound from the outdoor pool. Who could be swimming at night?

There it was again! Not a splash but a very big sneeze! Quickly Smooth climbed the wall that surrounded the pool. What she saw, as she pulled herself high enough to look over the top, almost made her fall back down again. Four round green eyes shone up at her. Water bobbed around four nostrils.

"Smooth," she heard, faint and sniffy.

Jumping down onto the poolside, Smooth drew closer to the water. By moonlight she saw that her parents filled the pool. It was such a tight squeeze for two dragons that their tummies almost touched. They could hardly move.

Cloud sneezed again.

"If you pushed really hard, couldn't you lift off," asked Smooth, "shake off the water and fly?"

Sadly the dragons shook their heads, spraying Smooth. She heard the clink of chains underwater – around their dragon feet. So cruel! Smooth felt angry and helpless. Spell had told her once that dragons didn't really hate water; they just couldn't defeat it.

But she could!

"I know!" she told them. "It'll be all right."

Smooth made her way in the darkness to the hut at the side of the pool. Feeling her way in, she trusted her hands to guide her. It must be here. Only days ago the caretaker and his team had drained the pool, cleaned it and filled it again. The water had to be nice and fresh for Lavelle's lesson. She was the best swimmer in the school.

Smooth stumbled as her legs found the coil of hose. A scrape of rubber never hurt anyone. Now where was the pump?

*

Emptying the pool was much more tiring than swimming could ever be. It was hard, sweaty work for a dragons' daughter who didn't have dragon muscles. Slowly, so slowly, the water level dropped – down to her parents' shoulders, their chests, their tummies…

Now the sun rose and trickled light through the skies. For the first time Smooth could see the water rush down to the sports fields. And for the first time she could see her parents clearly. Their wet scales crinkled, they huddled together. They were shivering. But otherwise they were quite still. It was as if they had shrunk in the water, and all their fun and energy had been drained away. Even their dragon eyes looked a faint, dull green in the morning light.

"Rest, Smooth," said Cloud, his voice faint.

Smooth could have sunk to the ground but she mustn't stop. Soon Mr and Mrs Highcastle would be awake. The lights would go on in the school and it would be too late…

Looking back to the bedroom windows, Smooth imagined Jack. She pictured him in his bed, waking and knowing. She was a dragons' daughter. She could make him understand.

Smooth sighed. Turning back to the pool, she breathed deeply. If she must do it alone, then she would. Nothing could stop her. On and on she worked, but soon the water looked as tired as she felt. It was more of a stream than a river now.

"Smooth!" she heard.

Her chest tightened with panic. But it wasn't Mr Highcastle. It was someone smaller but much braver.

"Let me help," said Jack.

For a boy who couldn't read yet, Jack had amazing strength. He had determination too. Now the water cleared twice as fast. Breathless, Smooth didn't hear the other footsteps following Jack onto the poolside. Spell saw first, and weakly waved her tail.

They were all in their nightshirts or pyjamas. The first child brought a bucket. The second had a biscuit tin. The third and fourth both carried saucepans. Now Smooth was the caretaker (of her dragon parents) and this was her team. A moment later they stood, one on each step down to the water. One after another the containers were filled and passed up to the poolside.

Before long the water level was down to the dragons' legs. Smooth could see the chains around their ankles. But she must keep her hand to the pump.

"Smooth!" cried Cloud. His voice sounded urgent – almost afraid.

Smooth looked; Jack looked. From the steps of the pool the children looked too. What they saw was a girl in a nightdress, tying her long, beautiful hair into a ponytail. Lavelle!

Had she told? Was it over?

Lavelle looked at the dragons, their skin tinged with blue and their claws shaking. She ran to the pool and dived in.

*

Down Lavelle swam, her nightdress streaming beneath the surface. The dragons were so cold under the water that their ankles had shrunk just a little. The chains were looser now. Gently Lavelle lifted Spell's feet from the floor of the pool and eased them through. Free, Spell wriggled upwards, aiming for the sky. But where was her dragon power? Still the water held her down. As Lavelle freed Cloud, he tried to spring up and out of the shallows. But instead he flopped back down again with a splash.

Smooth dropped the pump. "We have to warm them up," she said.

The sun was rising fast but they couldn't wait for it to warm the shivery dragon scales. Wading through the water, the children surrounded the dragons. They wrapped them in dressing gowns. With their hands they rubbed their backs and their tummies. They rubbed the front legs they held out of the water, like dogs hoping for a treat.

Jack climbed onto Cloud's head until his legs dangled down past the stiff dragon ears. He rubbed the top, the snout and the sunken cheeks. Smooth put her arms around Spell's neck and stroked it all the way up and down. Lavelle used her hair like the softest towel. Gradually the shrivelled dragons began to swell. Soon they gleamed again. All around the pool, on the bushes and branches, the birds began to sing.

Then all heads turned as the school filled with light and sound.

"No!" cried Smooth.

Shouts burst out. People were running. The caretaker and his team would have more darts to fire, more chains, a net...

The roar was louder than any human noise. It came from the thick green throat of Spell Dragon. Spreading her wings, she surged upwards, showering the children with water droplets and draping them with dressing gowns.

Up sprang Cloud Dragon, with the smallest boy in school on his head. Smooth watched. Had they forgotten her? Were they leaving without her?

With a twisting nosedive, Spell plunged down for her daughter. Up on her toes, Smooth stretched out an arm but it didn't reach. Behind her, the darts were being loaded. Any second now, they would fire again.

"Go!" yelled Smooth. "Go now!"

Spell had no choice. Bursting upwards, she chased after Cloud and Jack. Following each dart and swerve, Smooth kept her eyes on her dragon parents. Green again, they soared into the pale blue of the morning sky. Beneath them the children cheered. High above the school the dragons flew, with banners of fire curling after them.

Smooth stood and watched the sky. Her dragon parents were free again. And the nest would be a perfect fit for Jack.

"You!" cried an angry voice. Mr Highcastle waved a fist. "Smooth Dragon! I need to see you in my office now!"

Smooth ran. But no one followed. The caretaker tried, and so did his team, but each of them found a child in the way. Clinging to ankles and pulling on legs, the children wouldn't be shaken off. Not until Smooth Dragon was a long way up the fire escape.

Climbing fast, Smooth didn't look down. Everything she loved was above. Step after step she drew closer to the roof and the clock tower with its giant face. A light breeze cooled her but the sun felt soft on her skin. Almost there.

Smooth looked up but they were far away now, heading for the mountains. In her heart she knew she wasn't theirs. They had saved her from a blaze when she was tiny. It was what dragons did. In her dreams she'd felt them reach their dragon wings around her as she lay in her cot. She knew she was the baby they couldn't give away because they loved her too much. And she knew they'd always love her.

Tall and still, Smooth waited for the wind. As it came for her, she spread her arms like wings. Fearless, she reached up and let it lift her away. Gliding, then soaring, she had never felt so smooth.

The dragons' daughter was going home.

A piece written late October 2022 after being poorly

Feeling the Heat

It's day eleven. At last I went for a walk. The paths were dark, the shadows pale. I was slow, wondering at the stewed apple mush of sodden leaves beneath my tread. It shouldn't be so warm. Crossing to the playing fields, I thought how dead a house can look when its outline is edges; how secretly small histories pulse. How sad to find a tree I know so well to be a beacon blazing from higher ground when it's stooping and drained. Wondering how a fence can look so young when it's dead, but knowing it won't stop feeding. Watching leaves drift thinner and harder than snow. Wincing at the banner's call to Level Up with the Army; it must be white poppy time.

There's a small part of me that hates whoever fixed the mangled water bottle into the fence, and the company that made it. A part that regrets the angles, the pathos of pots on a bed of slate. I'm awed by roots writhing wild through sloping mud, and smile because oversized dandelions just keep on, rebirth after fragmentation, season-blind. The light is tender. Gold leaves gather dense and glowing, cast off yet newborn. I don't know what turns a wall to turmeric. And in the cemetery I wonder who Belinda was, because a hundred and three years later a careful blaze of petunias in freshly surfaced earth don't forget.

The Countess looms, taller, whiter, leaving space beneath for plebs to bow. Others are erased. One grave's dislodged, as if below the undead tried vainly to erupt. There's evidence of care, respect for the lost and unfound, of tending and honouring and curiosity, and I wonder why we are more willing to invest in the past than our future. Aware that comparing cedars to cavolo nero is a betrayal of privilege, I'm shamed by loving unknown trees because that's denying each its character and story. There's one that's a forest with fourteen trunks, every one unremarked. A man in summer clothes clinging with rain or sweat tells me his dog likes me, and walking warily away I suggest that's the colourful leggings, but he tells me dogs see in black and white and I think, No? Even in autumn? And isn't it sad that I don't trust men anymore when I'm alone?

It shouldn't be this warm. Admiring the ivy burst in a smart wall by the grand new gates, I wish it wasn't over. But there's a plant I can't name, probably a weed, sprouting so fine where the dereliction starts that the tiny yellow flowers seem magically suspended. I see the high street, smell lunches, coffee, smoke and sweetness, and wish the quiet could hold – but not as much as I long for the truth to break it. Turning up the hill I scorn the tat that clogs the real and green with unsustainable Hallowe'en waste. Then mini skeletons climbing a drainpipe almost win me over with echoes of cinema less knowing, from a time when we dared look up. I'm tired now as I near home – understanding suddenly that it isn't that, and never will be, because that was the house Dad drew, with the garden he sculpted and loved, where there was no grieving, at least not for me. Anne Michaels wrote, "All grief – anyone's grief – is the weight of a sleeping child," and that's meaningless and laden with meaning only feeling knows.

It's way too warm.

Our Nature
poem written having watched A Winter Walk with Lemn Sissay,* November 2022

When Dad's big hand closed around mine
I entered into the hush we shared with trees
to love what he loved,
to hold the peace we really breathed.
But I think I preferred Robin Hood fast-fighting the Sheriff
up spiralling stone stairs,
or colouring in Flower Fairies
and a sister's search through snow to break the magic
with bravest love.
Earth was dirt and sand between my toes to be scoured with no mercy.
I was afraid of a darkness
that flooded too soon and carried no candles,
of kept animals with stares to crush
and the wild ones that hid where imagination was free.
There's a time when brightness blinds with rhythm and walls seem enough
unless the sky is deeper blue and the sand dazzles,
and a time when children remind us of puddles and stones and
birds to hear before bedtime, or rain.
But it's only now, late, when knees need bolstering
feet misjudge roots
and negotiable space has shrunk like an old balloon,
now that the end flares and rushes, cracks and folds
and fills the void with mourning without voice,
that I feel Dad's love,
and grieve and glow and break
and belong,
that I'm thankful for TV to take me
where nature won't allow me to think
*I am the biggest story in my world.**
Only we are, together.
We write the next series
without understanding it could be the last.

statement made in court, August 2022, following arrest for aggravated trespass at Buncefield Oil Depot

I'm pleading guilty simply because as a grandma committed to regular childcare I don't want to lose another week in court. But my activism is childcare too and I stand by it. We are at a point in human history where every choice we make, as governments, corporations and individuals, increases or reduces our chances of survival as a species on this planet. No one can stop the harm in one day and save life on earth in the process, but we can all do what we can, peacefully and with love, to protect life. That's why I am a flight-free vegan, buy clothes from charity shops, try to shop zero waste, bank with Triodos and am a long-term customer of Good Energy. But after years of lawful campaigning I became a climate activist in 2018 because this isn't enough. Stopping the harm means resisting the fossil fuel companies that the UN Secretary General says have humanity "by the throat." Their influence on governments and media is so powerful that there were more representatives of that industry at COP26 than there were indigenous people calling desperately for help. Unless responsible citizens who respect the scientific consensus do everything we can, peacefully, to prevent new oil, gas and coal projects – in spite of The International Energy Authority's insistence that there can BE no such projects if we are to avert catastrophic climate and societal breakdown – my grandchildren will experience horrors I don't want to imagine. Children in the global south are already suffering and dying because of our emissions, not theirs. Because of our addiction to fossil fuels and our entitlement. We are seeing record temperatures and ice loss; recent wildfires around Europe and here in London give visible, visceral meaning to the **Gutteres'** phrase, Code Red for humanity. And not far from where I live there is an oil terminal with a pipeline to Heathrow, facilitating an industry that allows people in this country to exceed an individual's yearly sustainable carbon budget in one flight.

Blockading Buncefield on 1st April was more than a protest. It was a symbolic act, a way of telling the oil industry what activists told Shell at their AGM recently: "We will, we will stop you." And it was an act of love, on behalf of those most vulnerable in this crisis, who are the least heard. I have a placard that reads: BIG EMITTERS FLYING means LOW EMITTERS

DYING. My action was a way of stopping just some of the harm, just for one day. Of showing the industry, and the government that supports new excavation in defiance of the Paris Agreement, that we cannot give up on a liveable future. Of alerting the public misled by greenwash into thinking everything is under control. Of encouraging others within our various social circles who know the truth to live by it. No one protest can transform government policy, industry strategy or public opinion, but I have to hope that the cumulative impact of such direct action, which has already shifted the Overton Window, could lay the foundations of change.

As a Quaker and follower of Jesus, I was led by my conscience to blockade Buncefield. Any inconvenience caused shrinks into truly minor insignificance in the context of the sixth mass extinction for which scientists tell us we and most other species on this earth are heading. As the UN Secretary General has said, governments failing to curb fossil fuels are the dangerous radicals, not nonviolent protesters like me. The legal system cannot continue to criminalise those who act on the truth. It's just a matter of time, but that devastating truth tells us just how little of that we have left.

My Prison Diary

Day One

Thursday 15th September: from Oldbury Police Station to HMP Bronzefield via the Royal Courts of Justice

Having slept well in my police cell I woke to gruff news that I was going to court. No breakfast and no drink. The journey to the Royal Courts of Justice in Holborn took five hours thanks to rerouting due either to royally closed roads or a primitive satnav.

As we entered the bowels of the RCJ I was reminded of dungeons. The contrast with the grace and flourish of the ground level (with its high ceilings, oak panelling and rows of old hardback books so evenly sized that they might only have been colourful, if faded, wallpaper) was striking, a kind of physical symbol of inequality. But four of us, all vegans, shared a spirited cell, and the staff were gloriously friendly and eager to feed us. When the veggie curry turned out to contain milk we made do with stickily solid rice and black tea. We were then called up to court first, along with V and R. The judge didn't seem fazed by our joint failure to stand for him when he arrived. Neither did he attempt to stop us delivering our statements of non-compliance; in fact he said he appreciated us being concise. My legs had begun shaking from the time we sat down, and although I tried deep breaths their vibrations were for a while unstoppable – until we'd left the courtroom on remand up to our committal dates the following week. I was enormously relieved that mine was to be on the Tuesday.

On return to our group cell we must have appeared perversely elated, because we had expected remand and hoped it would make news as much as anything relating to commoners could at this time. After all there were 51 of us being sent to prison at once – some of whom we waved off and back to court as they made their way down the basement corridor. There has been a huge amount of waiting in my life in the last week, in this case to set off for HMP Bronzefield, which were told was "near Heathrow".

Although this was a quicker drive, we didn't arrive until about 7:30 p.m., after which we spent many more hours in the Reception area: searched, (fore)fingerprint taken for access to the pod along with a photo for the ID card, conversations with nurses and in my case a doctor too. I mentioned my dietary needs at every opportunity. Almost all of us are vegan but I was the only one to throw in gluten intolerance. Sitting in comfort on plastic sofa, looking at walls papered with soothing and beautiful views of autumn woods/coastline, chatting and being looked after by prisoner volunteers who welcomed us like family, we heard that Bronzefield is in some ways like "a Holiday Inn". But eating our vegan ready meals and drinking our coffees with oat milk, we were prevented from developing unrealistic expectations by T, who had been inside before. The volunteers in their red sweat jackets, who gave us string kit bags and answered questions, made it impossible to imagine them committing any crime. The youngest of them, who has three years remaining, assured us that vegan food would be provided and said she would join the movement when she gets out. In the kit bags were charcoal grey uniform items of T-shirt, sweatshirt, socks and joggers, plus generous but pretty knickers; plastic plate, cup, bowl and cutlery and one flask for boiling water, another for cold; soap, deodorant, sanitary supplies; colouring and activity sheets and an information booklet. Because we arrived so late and were so many, the normal reception process couldn't be completed but we were told the rest would happen the following day. We were also warned, though, that the timing, with a Bank Holiday weekend for the Queen's funeral, was the "wrong" one, and it was soon very obvious that underfunding and understaffing result in a system under pressure, in which staff feel stressed and prisoners demoralised at best.

I was lucky, allocated a cell sometime after one a.m; others had to wait several more hours. This was when reality struck as the door was locked behind us. Our cell was cramped, and a typically grim toilet greeted us. Otherwise we had shelving, a small TV on a long surface to use as a table, two plastic chairs and a drop-down blind that fell away from its Velcro fastening when touched – mysteriously shedding tampons! The barred window gave us a view of the exercise area, beyond which the height of the fences and their deterrent wire tips reminded me of wartime POW dramas. But I was paired with J, whom I knew and liked from the Buncefield action. Being five years younger than me and sportier, she offered to take the top bunk. Not for the first time, I felt a little overwhelmed by a situation that seemed surreal and shocking, but I was cosy under a duvet in my (rather cute) pink T-shirt prison nightie, hoping my snoring didn't disturb her as I crashed out until breakfast. I knew I could do this, and I knew that people must.

Day Two

Friday 16th September: new kids on the block

J and I both slept solidly for the six hours that remained once we'd been allocated the cell. I developed a novel washing routine thanks to the sanitary towels provided, using one instead of the flannel still in my backpack at Reception. (That was J's idea; she was already using one on a step up to the bunk, because nothing's very clean.) Around eight we were let out into the communal area for 10 – 15 minutes, shown up as newbies – and in my case by my shivering – in our prison nighties and bare feet. Two of the inmates immediately brought us bright pink flip-flops. Breakfast is a choice of two cereals and a piece of toast with jam, so nothing I could eat but J said someone who had already been on remand recommended sunflower spread, available in mini pots, as moisturiser. It didn't taste too oily on my lips, which were already ribboning without their usual 15 lip salve applications per day.

Our prisoner guides from the night before appeared to show us how to use the pod for all purchases and requests but we found that (inexplicably) it wouldn't accept my fingerprint. The others reported that because our cash hadn't been processed we weren't authorised in any case to use it for anything, including phone credit – in the ongoing absence of our one free call. The property check we expected didn't happen, but thankfully we had been allowed to take books in with us, (which we'd understood isn't allowed at most prisons in case the pages are impregnated with drugs???) I kept pressing gently for a gluten-free pack. Lunch for me was chips and mushy peas, but a particularly friendly long-term resident in the next cell gave me a couple of bananas. Sam, who is trans and presents as absolutely male from his build to walk, gestures, voice and Mohican, told us to come to him if we needed any help with anything. At some point a Chaplain came to see us, filled in forms and gave us some reading material and activity sheets. He said all the failings of the system go right "up to Number 10."

The sun shone all day, and sitting by the window I basked in it. J and I have different body thermostats; she cooled off in the T-shirt, rolling up her sleeves and jogger legs like the hillwalking cyclist she is, but I was grateful for layers. We were glad to be able to use the shower room which has two cubicles and one bath. I was reminded of a word my kids used as teenagers: skanky. But that didn't stop me celebrating! We both really enjoyed our time outside, in a bare kind of courtyard with grass at the centre where we could catch up with H from upstairs. Having initially been on her own because we were an odd number, she had now been given a cellmate who vaped, and felt obliged to say when asked that she didn't mind. We all hoped that would work out but it made me even more thankful to be with J. Again the three of us stood out from the crowd, this time by walking brisk, purposeful circuits while most who went out at all just sat on the stone benches. We were still pacing when we realised we were the only ones left and had been overlooked. We were locked out! We found this funny although the officer's reaction to our knocking implied that we were somehow to blame.

So we were only just in time for supper: in my case, sweetcorn, lettuce, tomato and cucumber, plus a pear and one of Sam's bananas. I realised that my dysfunctional guts were quiet without much to bother them. Although we'd understood that everyone is entitled to a free call within 24 hours, it was obvious now that it wasn't going to happen for us, and that was a real blow, knowing that everyone I love would be waiting anxiously by the phone and that without my prisoner number Leslie couldn't share it with anyone wanting to email. Even though I'd been calm and positive all day, and agreed when H said how aware she felt of her privilege because so many of our neighbours had such challenging issues, I was desperate to hear Leslie's voice, and worried for him and for Mum.

Weekend hours meant lock-up at about 4:30 p.m. with a "Goodnight, ladies." After a couple of quiz shows on TV, some deep talk and a little exhausted reading, I fell asleep very quickly, remembering all the good things of the day and the importance of recognising them, however small they might be. I felt loved, and told myself the wheels of the underfunded, understaffed system might clunk an inch or two forward tomorrow.

Day Three

Saturday 17th September: reaching the outside world

No breakfast except a banana but I queued for medication for the first time, and towards lunchtime we were allowed, after pestering, to make our free phone calls so the day became wonderful, if emotional. I cried when Leslie picked up; it felt overwhelming. There was so much to say and so little time before I was cut off early, after assuring him, "But the important thing to tell you is that I'm OK." I was relieved to hear that Mum was "taking it well" and that he'd held her hand while she read my letter, written before I left for Birmingham. H's husband told her that given the situation with the Queen we'd received some good coverage and would otherwise have made the front page. We were jubilant, and thrilled to hear that an open letter from 150 barristers had been published, criticising the government's unlawful energy policy and the prosecution of those who oppose it. Katie, the young, highly tattooed officer who had given us the opportunity to use the phone, really seemed determined to make it happen so we were very grateful.

Lunch for me was baked beans and hash brownies and I was so hungry that although it wasn't very hot first time round I did hurry back for "Seconds!" Protein at last! Sam kindly spent some money from his own account ordering some peanut butter for me on the pod, on the off chance that it would arrive before I left. And another prisoner gave us each a soya yogurt because she's lactose-free and our vegan packs still hadn't materialised.

In the early afternoon we discovered National Prison Radio on our television, and danced to Status Quo before the music turned to slush. It was requests day and many loved ones had called in from outside. We thought how great it would be for climate prisoners to hear such a message, followed perhaps by Blythe Pepino's *Emergency*. We also wondered how soon printed email messages would appear under our door. H told us once we met outside under another blue sky that her asthma was being aggravated by her cellmate's vaping, and that she believed she was inside for violent crime. Outdoor conversation about time remaining yielded the claim from one prisoner that during their last spell inside they'd looked ahead by writing KILL on the calendar on the day after release. This was when it hit home that some of our neighbours were dangerous. Many, though, were interested in why we were there, opening up the opportunity for truth telling about climate. There was general outrage or disbelief that we could be imprisoned for protest.

I asked whether H could be moved but was told that would be a problem because "everyone" vaped. Permanent pressure makes the staff seem dismissive and sometimes irritated when asked for anything. I felt for H, who is so gentle. For tea I had lettuce, cucumber and carrot, a pear and another soya yogurt. By this point I had learned that there was always a queue for the pod, and that those waiting in it were often sacrificing a shower, a laundry opportunity or a chance to empty their bin, because there wasn't time for everything. I was beginning to question the hygiene regime of washing plates in our cell basin with a little soap; my mug was becoming stained by all the black tea or coffee. We're still requesting vegan packs every time the door is unlocked.

Simon Reeve in South America, while fascinating, showed us devastating environmental destruction for gold and oil. I kept colouring as I watched, planning to complete three designs, one each for my grandchildren. J and I discovered a shared affection for Janis Ian, Davy Jones and Follyfoot, and we'd both seen Joan Armatrading in concert. She read until ten again but I crashed out earlier, undisturbed by the light and smiling at the memory of Leslie's voice.

Day Four

Sunday 18th September: Sunday service

Overnight there had been a fight in a cell near ours, with yelling and the clatter of chairs being thrown, but the noise subsided eventually. Breakfast for me consisted of two donated soya yogurts. But later the lactose-free prisoner gave J a little carton of soya milk which she passed on to me because her veganism isn't, in this context, as hard-core as mine. Another small blessing to appreciate: a white, fairly hot coffee. Sadly, and mysteriously in view of medication security, we heard that a prisoner had gone to hospital in the night with an overdose.

J began to have tooth trouble and the pain increased through the day, especially when she ate, but no doctor was available on a Sunday and she was warned against requesting a dentist described as a butcher by other prisoners. Animated and open conversation was interrupted, as we waited for Chapel, by the key in the lock – but J's name was on the list; mine wasn't. I assumed this was a muddle, but it happened because J, tipped off that Chapel represented an outing, had put Christian on her form and I'd written Quaker! I decided to embrace the time for solo worship of the Quaker kind, so I moved my chair to face the sunlight through the window and entered into the silence, practising gratitude and praying for others as well as trying to clear space to receive insight. It felt beautiful.

I was called from the glowing quiet for meds, and asked for Paracetemol on top so that J didn't miss her chance at Chapel. My plan was to bring the tablets back, not realising that I'd be required to swallow them in front of the pharmacist and then open my mouth to prove them gone. In fact J was able to pick up painkillers on her way back from the service, where she'd been moved by three visiting gospel singers and found me doing my faux-ballet moves at the end of the corridor where I was largely hidden from view. Then a different kind of dancing broke out, and we joined in – welcomed with smiles, laughter and comments like, "Go, girl!" The music from a CD player wasn't my genre of choice but I really enjoyed it, and a couple of the officers caused hilarity with a few moments of boogie. One lunch option was nut roast which I couldn't eat because of the breadcrumbs, so I made do with roast potatoes and carrots, until a bean salad was produced – by which I mean the usual straggly lettuce, tomato and cucumber with cold mixed beans from a can. I saved most of that for later, preferring another soya yogurt.

As well as pursuing food packs we continued to ask whether money had made it into our accounts, or whether we might be called out for a property check, but were told we'd have to wait now until after the weekend.

Later in the afternoon, H appeared at my door the moment it was unlocked and asked to come in. Crying, she explained that her cellmate kept threatening to harm her, and herself. She had come to prison from a mental hospital and H thought she probably didn't mean it but I determined to advocate for her, and eventually succeeded in signalling through the bars to a senior officer in the central office until I was allowed through. Leslie calls the braver, more assertive me "XR Sue" and I needed her. Result! Within half an hour H had a new cellmate: JSO's M from the wing opposite. More relief and delight. And J's painkillers were working.

Noticing me coming away from the serving hatch at tea with a pear, one warden we hadn't seen before went off on a declared mission to find me food, asking every prisoner if they had anything gluten-free. The outcome was a pack of hula hoops – a treat quickly despatched – and the end of a packet of Free From Corn Flakes. Delighted and touched, I looked forward to my first prison breakfast.

Day Five

Monday 19th September

J's tooth infection had really flared up overnight, depriving her of sleep, so the priority of the day was getting medical help: more Paracetemol, only available to be swallowed on the spot at certain times. My gluten-free Corn Flakes with soya milk tasted ten times better than they could have done in the free world! J hoovered the floor of charcoal fluff; I mopped. And catching up with M, H's new cellmate, it was great to find H smiling. When J and I handed in our laundry bags, we were told that they couldn't include underwear so I washed my prison knickers with soap in our basin. With absolutely nowhere to dry them in the cell, I hung them from the latch of the open window behind bars in the communal corridor, not sure what I'd do if instructed to remove them. I don't think anyone noticed, any more than anyone bothered about the litter below.

At last I was called by Solomon, a lovely officer from Reception, to go for my property check. I pointed out that J should go before me because she wasn't due in court until Friday. He told me to fetch her too, and we found two other protesters waiting there. I was only allowed to keep certain clothes items including my oldest, most dispensable knickers and character references I didn't expect to be read. Not the lip salve I craved or the zero-waste face bar. (My skin had developed rashes on the face and thighs.) "Could I just apply them once in front of you?" I asked the two guys, who seemed kind. One told me with a grin that I was "really pushing it"; the other closed his eyes. Humanity wins over regulation! Having gone first and while waiting for us all to be processed, J discovered some emails on the pod and was overcome by the number even though there wasn't much time to skim through them all. I hoped that against the odds I could access mine even though I knew how emotional that would be, but my fingerprint continued to block me so I couldn't even transfer money (finally available) over to the phone account. The others, who did, were warned that there would be further delay before they could pick up the receiver.

My vegan pack came good at lunchtime when I ate new potatoes and peas, more donated Corn Flakes and a soya yogurt. We ignored the funeral coverage no one seemed to be talking about, and filled the afternoon with colouring and personal storytelling. Once allowed out we somehow missed the shout for fresh air so exercised in the corridor instead, together doing the PEACE, LOVE, TRUTH, JUSTICE mantra with moves that I'd shown J the day before. There was another spontaneous disco before lock-up, but briefer and smaller, with only three of us dancing. Tea brought me Mexican bean salad AND a gluten-free sandwich with vegan cheese. For the first time I felt as if I'd eaten enough and my guts remained subdued.

Paddington 2 was Film on 4 and on finding it I may have whooped or punched the air. It was a perfect start to the night before my court appearance, but later I did lie awake telling myself that if necessary I *could* do another week in prison, or ten days, or even a fortnight. I half-believed it. My fear was for Leslie and Mum, Philip and Sarah, and that any sentence would be served – as we'd been warned – in another prison where I might share with a stranger and where I would start at the beginning again with dietary requests.

Overnight J was in agony so I buzzed for painkillers, asking also whether the court schedule had confirmed a physical appearance for me or just a video link, because I'd been told they would let me know by 10 p.m. They couldn't, and I forgot to ask when J had to buzz again at three a.m. I was distressed for her and sorry that if I left her it would be in pain.

Day Six

Tuesday 20th September

Woken at 6:20, I was given ten minutes to wash, dress and bag up, and couldn't retrieve my laundry before I left J with a big, full hug. C and I had to wait in Reception with two other prisoners for what turned out to be more than two hours, in my case without breakfast because the only option was toast and jam. The space was dominated by someone young, endearing, funny, vulnerable, damaged and scary who swung a thick green elastic thread as she lounged, and could be a huge character in a story except that I wouldn't dare guess the life experiences she's had. Her chat focused at one point on a named prisoner she avoided, who had driven with a severed head on her passenger seat. Once the long white van with its little individual cells finally left, we soon stopped off at another prison, and on reaching Birmingham we circled past Matalan and the Salvation Army four or five times in search of the Crown Court. By the time we arrived early in the afternoon I was finding the hunger, along with nervous preparation for a bad outcome, disturbing. Being a fainter I thought I might pass out in or before court, even after I was brought THREE packets of crisps.

The crown court cell was considerably grottier than at the Law Courts in London and the wait seemed longer on my own, but I finished *Blessed Unrest*, wishing I had a pen to mark everything I learned so I couldn't lose it. (I'd left J my all-time favourite novel, *Let Me Tell You About A Man I Knew* by Susan Fletcher.) For the first time since speaking to Leslie, I shed some tears – thanks to the young and empathetic prosecuting lawyer who gave me a wodge of papers with the assurance that I'd go in last to allow me time to read them. That was a task I had zero strength to undertake. I told her about my lack of food and even though I wished I'd stayed strong (XR Sue deserted me there) it paid off because I was eventually called in as part of the second group of defendants. Leslie, who was one of about fifteen observers, had overheard the judge being told that I was unwell.

Along with two JSO women who'd been on remand at Foston Hall, I faced Judge Kelly from a distance and behind Perspex, in a much more functional and less ancient courtroom than in Holborn. After technical hitches with earpieces, a lot of repetition and considerable exaggeration of disruption and danger, I was given a suspended sentence of another 25 days, which I will only have to serve if I break the injunction again during the next two years. The judge appeared unmoved by our three mitigation statements and as she summed up, beginning with a custodial sentence and working downwards, I'd feared the worst, so the relief was enormous. We each have to pay £416 costs.

There was still some time to wait before I was actually released from the court cell but thankfully I was given a vegan, g-f lasagne which substituted convincingly for manna from heaven. I didn't let go of Leslie all the protracted train journey home, during which we had a conversation with a supportive passenger. I was saddened to learn that Rajan, who had broken the injunction for the third time, had been given another 34 days, but he is deeply spiritual with huge dignity and awe-inspiring commitment and strength.

It's been a big experience and not one I want to repeat. I've assured my loved ones and myself that I won't take the risk. But I have absolutely no regrets. Reading all the many messages from friends and strangers, including one from a police officer also a mum, I was glad to see that it's led others to the conclusion that they need to do more themselves. Just one of the 170 fossil fuel projects planned by the government – the Jackdaw gas field – will have the emissions of GHANA.

It's beyond wonderful to be home.

poem written in HMP Bronzefield, Sept 2022

Inside

Once the lock clangs open
I dance alone,
obscured by billiard table and bookshelf
in the sunlight by the bars
where an old, stiff cobweb glints
like the wire looping high into bright sky outside.
At the foot of the fence old litter clings.
Nothing happens fast.
Requests are adjourned, sidelined, forgotten.
Still the refusnik phone in my cell
lies unconnected
to the cash they counted at Reception
And I could cry but I won't,
because I'm far too blessed.
I wear my privilege like a cross.
Hearing music, I dare to strut some stuff,
grin when the officers boogie too,
wonder whether this
is the good thing for today,
a day when I haven't used
words like climate, oil, floods and emissions.
But the baths haven't erased them from my skin
or shifted them from the deepest place
where they lodge and stab
with light.

www.ingramcontent.com/pod-product-compliance
Lightning Source LLC
Chambersburg PA
CBHW060336260626
47160CB00007B/2809